DATE DUE   FEB 04

GAYLORD   PRINTED IN U.S.A.

DANGER: DYNAMITE!

For my mother,
Margaret Conroy Capeci,
and for my uncle,
David James Conroy

CP
JR

A Peachtree Junior Publication

Published by
PEACHTREE PUBLISHERS, LTD.
1700 Chattahoochee Avenue
Atlanta, Georgia 30318-2112

www.peachtree-online.com

Text © 2003 by Anne Capeci
Illustrations © 2003 by Paul Casale

Book design by Loraine M. Joyner and Regina Dalton-Fischel
Composition by Melanie M. McMahon

Manufactured in China
10 9 8 7 6 5 4 3 2 1
First Edition

ISBN 1-56145-288-2

Library of Congress Cataloging-in-Publication Data

Capeci, Anne.
  Danger, dynamite! / written by Anne Capeci ; illustrated by Paul Casale.-- 1st ed.
    p. cm. -- (The Cascade mountain mysteries ; bk. 1)
  Summary: Ten-year-old Billy, his best friend Finn, and a girl named Dannie, living in a 1920s camp of railroad workers in the Cascade Mountains, follow clues to try to uncover the relationship of a stolen crate of dynamite with gold taken during an 1893 train robbery.
  ISBN 1-56145-288-2
  [1. Buried treasure--Fiction. 2. Cascade Range--Fiction. 3. Northwest, Pacific--History--20th century--Fiction. 4. Railroads--Trains--Fiction. 5. Mystery and detective stories.]
I. Casale, Paul, ill. II. Title.
  PZ7.C17363Dan 2003
  [Fic]--dc21
                                        2003006307

CASCADE MOUNTAIN

1

RAILROAD MYSTERIES

DANGER: DYNAMITE

ANNE CAPECI

PEACHTREE

Acknowledgments

The author would like to thank the following people for their invaluable help in researching and preparing this book: David Conroy, Margaret Conroy Capeci, and Elizabeth (Buffy) Rempel for the wonderful stories and memories that made this series possible; Pete Conroy, for generously allowing the use of his photographs; Eva Anderson, author of *Rails Across the Cascades,* which provided valuable historical information; Lisa Banim, for her expert guidance in helping to shape the story; and the Great Northern Railway Historical Society, for helping me to find detailed information about how the Cascade Tunnel was built.

Table of Contents

Chapter One
BIG PLANS

Scenic, Washington
1926

Billy Cole slumped in his chair. Why was the last hour in the school day always so long? It was torture to sit still. Especially when Alice Ann Lockhart was in the middle of one of her boring old poems.

"By the shores of Gitche Gumee," Alice Ann was saying. Her voice sounded high and prim. "By the shining Big-Sea-Water..."

Alice Ann was well into Henry Wadsworth Longfellow's famous poem *Song of Hiawatha*. She stood in front of the fourth-grade desks, tall and proud. She reminded Billy of the Douglas fir trees that grew on the mountain above the schoolhouse.

Alice Ann's chin-length blond hair was tucked neatly behind her ears. Every fold of her plaid skirt was perfectly in place. She probably thought there was only one reason they were all there in Scenic, Washington: to listen to her long, dull recitations.

Of course, Billy knew that wasn't true. The Great Northern Railway's new tunnel had brought his classmates and their families to the new Scenic camp. Men were working around the clock, seven days a week, to blast a path eight miles long through the Cascade Mountains. Every one of his friends in the two-room schoolhouse had a father or brother working a shift. Billy's own father was the general manager in charge of the whole project.

That was a big job. Billy swelled with pride every time he thought about his dad. He had begged to work in the tunnel himself. But his mother said that a ten-year-old boy belonged in school. So here he was, stuck listening to Alice Ann.

"There the wrinkled old Nokomis nursed the little Hiawatha..." Alice Ann went on.

The teacher, Miss Wrigley, sat at her desk at the front of the room. She nodded and smiled at Alice Ann. Billy rolled his eyes.

A soft breeze blew in through the open windows. Springtime had finally come to Scenic. Billy and his classmates no longer had to walk through snow that was over their heads to get to school. Now that the drifts had melted, the entire camp had sprung to life. Every blast of dynamite from inside the mountain tunnel made birds flap their wings and squirrels chatter in alarm.

"*Psst!*"

Billy glanced over his shoulder at his best pal, Finn Mackenzie. Finn sat right behind Billy. But Billy didn't dare turn around. If he did, he'd catch it from Miss Wrigley for sure. Their teacher had promised both boys a stiff punishment the next time they acted up in class.

"Knock-knock," Finn whispered.

Billy grinned. He and Finn had been friends since the moment they met. That was six months ago. Billy's mother had brought Billy and his little sister, Marjorie, to join their father in Scenic. The little town in the mountain wilderness was growing quickly. More men were arriving by the dozens every day to work.

Billy's father had promised him that the Tye River was full of plump trout waiting to be caught. That first day, Billy had rushed from his cabin with his fishing pole. And he found Finn waiting outside with *his* fishing pole.

Finn, his blue eyes twinkling from under a mop of bright red hair, hadn't even said hello. He'd just said, "Knock-knock."

It was the beginning of a fine friendship.

"Who's there?" Billy answered, just as he had that day.

"Orange," Finn whispered.

"Orange who?" Billy asked, playing along. He glanced back at Alice Ann. She was still droning on. And on.

"Orange you dying to get out of here?" Finn said. "We need to finish building our cannon!"

Billy turned his head toward the windows. He tried to get a glimpse of Lookout Rock, where their pine tree fort and cannon were waiting for them. But a large branch outside the window hid the big rock ledge, which jutted out of the mountainside above the school.

"We should pile up some rocks," he whispered to Finn, "so we can set the pipe at the right angle."

Wes Gundy, another one of their friends, heard him. "Hey, I've got some twine," he offered.

Wes had helped the boys build the fort. His pockets always bulged with marbles, bent nails, and string that he found around the camp. Wes and Billy shared a desk near the back of the fourth-grade row. The other girls in their class, Lucy Grinnell and Janet Kleig, sat in front of them. Alice Ann, of course, had a desk to herself at the front of the classroom. The first, second, and third graders sat at the other rows of desks. There was one grade to each row.

4

"I know what we can use for the launcher," Finn added. "There's an old inner tube in the trash heap behind the family cabins. I saw it yesterday."

"Perfect!" Billy said. "We can cut a strip of rubber and tie it on with—"

"Ahem!" Miss Wrigley cleared her throat.

Billy blinked. *Oops,* he thought.

"Billy Cole and Finn Mackenzie." Miss Wrigley sighed. "What am I going to do with you two boys?"

It did not sound like the teacher wanted an answer. Billy bit his lip and kept silent.

"Not only did you disrupt Alice Ann's splendid recitation of Mr. Longfellow's poem," Miss Wrigley scolded. "But you also interrupted the studies of the younger students in this classroom. I believe you owe everyone an apology."

Alice Ann stood behind Miss Wrigley, smirking at the boys.

"Sorry," Billy mumbled. He scraped the toe of his boot across the rough-cut floorboards.

"It won't happen again," Finn spoke up from his desk. "We promise."

"Oh, I think more than a promise is called for," Miss Wrigley said. "Now let me see..." She tapped her chin, thinking. "Why don't you start by wiping the blackboard after class? Then you can fill the coal bin and sweep the floor. And oh yes—I'd like you to tidy up the coatroom, too."

"Yes, ma'am," Billy and Finn said together. Billy's heart sank. Now it would be forever before they could get up to Lookout Rock!

A loud ringing sounded from the classroom next door. That was where Scenic's other teacher, Mr. Farnam, taught the students in grades five through eight. Billy saw Mr. Farnam step into the coatroom. He was swinging the bell he used to signal the beginning and end of each school day.

"Oh dear. Four o'clock so soon?" Miss Wrigley sighed. "Class is dismissed." She looked at Billy and Finn. "Boys, you may begin your extra chores."

The other students jumped up and hurried past Billy and Finn. Clomping feet and clattering lunch pails crashed through the coatroom. Soon voices could be heard outside.

Billy dragged himself to his feet. He knew exactly where to find the bucket and rags. This wasn't the first time he'd had to do chores after school.

Just then, Alice Ann passed outside the window. She tucked her books under her arm as Lucy and Janet fell into step next to her. The two other girls weren't quite as tall as Alice Ann. Or as bossy, either, Billy thought. Lucy was thin and quiet, with wispy brown hair and bangs. Janet was rounder, with black curls that fell just below her ears. Both girls wore skirts and sailor shirts exactly like Alice Ann's.

Alice spotted Billy watching her. She quickly stuck her tongue out at him. Then she said something to Lucy and Janet. The three of them ran off, laughing.

Billy scowled. "Hey, Finn," he said, as his friend came up beside him. Finn's hands were covered in chalk.

Finn glanced back at Miss Wrigley. The teacher was marking papers at her desk. "What?" he asked glumly.

"When we *do* finish our cannon," Billy said, "I know exactly where we'll shoot the first bag of dirt. Straight at Alice Ann Lockhart."

Chapter Two

DIRT BOMBS AND DYNAMITE

illy pushed the broom across the coatroom floor. Finn was on his knees, holding the dustpan. It felt like they had been cleaning up forever. Their hands were black from filling the coal bin. Billy's nose itched from all the dirt they had swept up.

The teacher appeared in the doorway. "All right, boys," she said. "You may go home now."

"Thanks, Miss Wrigley!" Finn said, jumping up. "See you Monday!"

The boys grabbed their books and lunch pails and burst through the schoolhouse door. But they didn't go home. They headed straight for Lookout Rock.

"Let's hurry!" Finn said. "Before Wes and his pals finish our cannon without us."

The boys leaped over a low fence. Billy saw a group of kids near the pine-branch walls of their fort. He recognized Wes's blue shirt and black hair. Next to him were Wes's big brother, Eddie, and Eddie's friend, Jim Walsh. Both boys were a year older and in Mr. Farnam's class.

Billy and Finn dumped their things in a heap at the foot of Lookout Rock and scrambled up the steep path. They reached the top in time to see Eddie tie a strip of rubber to the back of the pipe.

"Hey, hold on! That was *our* idea!" Finn called.

"So?" Eddie said, shrugging. He was crouched over the pipe in front of their fort. Wes and Jim were scraping dirt from the ground. They poured it into brown paper sacks at their feet.

"We've got the cannon almost ready. That's the important thing," Wes said.

"We'd never have finished if we'd waited for you," Eddie added.

That was true, thought Billy. He eyed the sun, which hung low in the western sky. In the fading light, he could see the whole camp: the schoolhouse and family cabins, the cookhouse and hospital and recreation hall, the bunkhouses and storage sheds and barns and machine shops. The jumble of buildings seemed to grow right out of the mountains. Many of them were so new that their tarpaper roofs had not yet been finished. The old ski lodge was about the only building that *wasn't* new. It had been a big hotel once. Now Billy's father had his office there, on the second floor. In the downstairs of the lodge were the camp store, the post office, the security office, and a barbershop.

Billy's eyes moved to the shining silver twin rails that curved around the edge of town. Twice a day, the Northern Express roared across them from the west with supplies from Skykomish and Seattle. After stopping at Scenic, they zigzagged up and over the Cascade Mountains in a series of switchbacks. The trains kept chugging east, past Wenatchee and Spokane, all the way to Chicago. Every time Billy heard a train's high, piercing whistle, he felt closer to those far-off places.

A faint boom echoed in the air, but Billy didn't flinch. He heard that sound all the time. With every blast of dynamite, the new tunnel was moving deeper into the mountain. Billy could hardly wait until the tunnel was finished. Then trains would be able to speed straight through the mountain. The slow-going switchbacks would be a thing of the past.

"Well...I guess the launcher looks all right." Finn stood behind Eddie and the cannon. He watched carefully while Eddie tied a knot to hold the launcher tight.

Billy nodded and walked over to them. "Let's try it out!" he said.

Wes and Jim had tied the dirt-filled sacks shut with twine.

"Catch!" Wes said. He threw a bag to Finn.

Finn set the dirt bomb bag against the rubber launcher. He dug the heels of his boots into the ground. Then he pulled the launcher back as far as it would go.

"Well, I don't see Alice Ann," he said, grinning at Billy. "But I bet we can hit the schoolhouse roof."

"Are you crazy?" Billy said. "If Miss Wrigley catches us..."

"Aw, she won't know anything about it," Jim said. "See? She's leaving now."

Billy glanced down from Lookout Rock. Miss Wrigley was just closing the door of the schoolhouse behind her. She walked briskly along the river, heading toward the family cabins. A moment later, she disappeared through the trees.

"Anyhow, *we* aren't going to bomb anything," Finn cut in. "The cannon will!"

With that, he let go of the launcher.

Zing!

The dirtball flew from the clay pipe like a shot. It sailed high into the air—farther than Billy could have dreamed possible.

"It's going right over the school!" Wes shouted.

The boys watched in awe as the cannonball disappeared over the far side of the schoolhouse roof.

"Jeepers!" Billy said excitedly. "That's a good fifty feet. Maybe even—"

Crash!

The sounds of breaking glass made Billy's words stop in his throat. The other boys' faces went pale.

"Uh-oh," Finn said. "Was that the shed window?"

All Billy could do was nod. They had forgotten about the tiny storage shed, tucked behind the schoolhouse.

"We're in hot water now," said Wes.

"Nope," Eddie said, with a firm shake of his head. "We won't get in trouble. Not if no one catches us."

He began to scramble down the side of Lookout Rock. The other boys ran after him. They slipped and slid down the steep path, then took off at a run.

"Hey, wait!" Billy called to Finn. He stopped in his tracks. "I just thought of something."

"What?" Finn asked, puffing a little.

"Miss Wrigley knows we're always up on Lookout Rock," said Billy. "When she sees that broken window, she'll know we did it! She might reckon we were trying to get back at her for those extra chores."

"Maybe we could fix it," Finn said slowly. "We could clean it up to look like nothing happened. Miss Wrigley never even has to know!"

"Let's go," Billy said.

He and Finn climbed over the fence and ran behind the schoolhouse. The storage shed stood between two tall pines. Billy gulped when he saw the jagged hole in the middle of the shed's only window. Pieces of glass littered the ground beneath it. Billy and Finn stepped carefully around the mess and pushed open the door.

As the boys stepped inside, fading sunlight filtered in through the broken window. It lit up dusty cobwebs and a jumble of supplies. Wood planks and rolls of tarpaper leaned against one wall. Metal cans, dripping with tar, were piled three high in a corner. An old desk stood in the center of the shed, with chairs and books stacked on top.

The cannonball had exploded on the desk. Dirt, glass, and bits of brown paper were everywhere. More dirt had splattered on the floor and in the bins of supplies. Now Billy wished Wes hadn't filled the sack quite so high with dirt.

"We'll never get all this cleaned up," he sighed. He kicked with his boot to clear dirt and glass from the top of a wooden crate. "We might as well–"

Billy broke off in mid-sentence. He stared at the words that were printed on the crate in big, red letters:

DANGER — HIGH EXPLO

A wedge-shaped piece of the crate was broken half off. It dangled to the side with the letters SIVES on it.

Billy had no trouble putting the two halves of the word together. "Explosives!" he cried.

His eyes flew to the hole in the wooden crate—and to the rows of powder-covered sticks stacked inside.

"Dynamite? For real?" Finn peered through the hole in the crate. His eyes went wide. Then fear crept into them.

"Billy," he whispered. "We sure picked the wrong place to shoot that cannonball."

Chapter Three
Now You See It...

Billy's heart pounded inside his chest. Goose bumps popped out on his arms and legs as he backed toward the door.

"We'll be blown up!" Finn whispered. He was still staring at the box of dynamite.

Billy and Finn both knew about the dangers of explosives. Finn's father was in charge of the powder crews. Those were the men who planted sticks of dynamite to blast the rock loose. A month earlier, a charge had gone off accidentally near the tunnel. Four men had lost their lives. Half a dozen more had been injured. Mr. Mackenzie was one of them. He walked with a limp now.

"N-no one's going to blow up," Billy said. But he wished he felt more sure about that. He grabbed Finn's sleeve and pulled him toward the door. Neither of them breathed until they were safely outside—and far away from the shed.

"What's that dynamite doing in there?" Finn said. "They always keep it locked up near the tunnel."

"I don't know," Billy said. "But we'd better tell someone quick."

"My father's not here," Finn said. "He had to see a man in Seattle about supplies today."

"My dad, then," Billy said.

Billy's father was the general manager at the camp. He was one of the top men on the job. If there was any kind of trouble, Mr. Cole was the person to see about it.

The boys walked quickly past the family cabins. Then they turned onto Scenic's only road. It ran along the railroad tracks. Billy didn't bother to stop at his father's office. His father was hardly ever there. Mr. Cole spent most of his time at the tunnel, where he could oversee the work himself.

The sun set as Finn and Billy hurried toward the tunnel entrance. Behind them, lights winked on all over Scenic. From the road, the boys could see men clomping in their boots up the stairs of the wooden walkways that ran between the buildings. Six feet high, the walkways made it easier to get around after heavy snows. There was already a crowd outside the cookhouse. Billy could smell beef and bread cooking. But the knot in his stomach kept him from feeling very hungry.

Up ahead, electric lights were strung along the wooden beams that framed the tunnel entrance. Half a dozen battered wagons sat on the rails outside. They were piled high with newly blasted granite. A crew of men was unloading the wagons. Their faces, hands, and clothes were smeared with dusty grime.

"Dad!" Billy called out.

Mr. Cole was talking to the foreman of the work crew. He had one boot propped on a pile of blasted rock. His thumbs were hooked through his belt loops.

"What is it, boys?" Mr. Cole asked. He said something to the foreman, and stepped away. He was frowning. Billy could read the message in his father's eyes. If they were interrupting his work, it had better be important.

"Dad, we found dynamite! A whole crate of it!" Billy told him.

He and Finn both started talking at once. Billy gulped a little when he and Finn told his father about the broken window. Luckily, Mr. Cole just raised his eyebrows and kept listening. But when they got to the part about finding the dynamite, his face grew darker than the shadows that were settling over the camp.

"There shouldn't be explosives anywhere near that school," Mr. Cole said. "I'd better have a look."

Mr. Cole asked one of the workers for a flashlight. Then he and the boys hurried back to the storage shed. Mr. Cole aimed the light at the jagged hole in the window.

"You boys stay here," he said.

He disappeared through the door of the shed. Billy watched the yellow beam dart around inside. His father's boots scraped across dirt and broken glass. Then came a series of thumping footsteps and Mr. Cole was back in the shed doorway.

"What kind of shenanigans are you two boys trying to pull?" he said.

His father's angry tone startled Billy. The flashlight beam hit him full in the face. Billy blinked. "W-what do you mean?" he asked.

"There's no dynamite in there," his father said. "None at all. The only suspicious things I saw were a broken window and a big mess. The mess you boys made when you shot that dirtball."

"But there is dynamite, Mr. Cole. We saw it!" Finn insisted.

"It's on the floor, Dad," Billy said. He ran to the shed, took the flashlight from his father, and shined it in. "Right next to—"

He gasped. In the spot where the crate had been, there was nothing but floorboards, dirt, and broken glass.

"It's gone!" he cried.

Finn ran up behind him. "But...how?" he asked.

"Boys," Mr. Cole said sternly. "A crate of dynamite doesn't just appear out of nowhere and then vanish again into thin air. If I find out you cooked up this whole story just to get out of trouble for breaking that window..."

"But Dad, we didn't!" Billy said.

"Honest, Mr. Cole." Finn pushed past Billy. "See?" he said, pointing to the floor next to the desk. "There's hardly any dirt. And that's the spot where the crate was."

Billy nodded. "There's just a little glass and some dirty streaks," he said. "Like someone dragged the crate to the door."

"Hey, I know!" Finn said. "Maybe we can find it again!"

"Sure!" said Billy. He and Finn started toward the door.

Mr. Cole blocked their way. "Not so fast, boys," he said, crossing his arms. "It seems to me the *real* trouble here was caused by a whole lot of foolishness with a sack of dirt."

Billy kicked at the floor. "We saw real dynamite," he mumbled. "Right here."

Mr. Cole's face remained stern. But when Billy glanced up, he noticed a glimmer of worry in his father's eyes. Mr. Cole scanned the shadowy corners of the shed once more. "Explosives are very dangerous," he said at last. "If there *are* any missing, you boys are not to go looking for them. You leave that to me. From now on, this shed is off limits. No one is to set foot inside. Understand?"

Billy and Finn nodded. They followed Mr. Cole outside.

"And I expect the two of you to march straight over to Miss Wrigley's cabin this minute and tell her what you've done," Billy's father went on. "I'm sure she'll think of a good punishment to make up for breaking that window."

Billy groaned. But he knew better than to argue with his father. "Yes, sir," he sighed.

He and Finn exchanged glances. They had only been trying to help. Now they were in worse trouble than ever!

Chapter Four

A CLUE IN THE TREES

I can't believe this," Finn complained the next morning. "A whole crate of dynamite is missing. And we can't do a thing about it!"

"Instead we get to do *more* chores," said Billy. He lugged a bucket of black paint into Mr. Farnam's classroom.

Finn followed behind him, carrying two brushes. "Yeah. On a Saturday."

They had already given the blackboard in Miss Wrigley's room a fresh coat of paint. Black splotches covered their skin and clothes, but they weren't done yet. Their teacher had been very clear. The blackboards in both classrooms were to be painted.

"Well, you heard my dad," Billy went on. He dipped his brush into the bucket. "No hunting for explosives."

"Right," Finn said. But Billy could tell that his friend wasn't happy.

By the time they went to clean their brushes near the river, it was early afternoon. Billy kneeled down to dip his brush into a jar of turpentine. He didn't see Wes, Eddie, and Jim until they sneaked up beside him and Finn.

"So you guys got caught?" Eddie asked. He picked up a pinecone and tossed it into the river. "What's the matter, couldn't you run fast enough?"

Finn used a rag to rub black paint from his hands and shirt. "We found a crate of dynamite."

"What?" Eddie, Jim, and Wes all cried at once.

The other boys stood with their mouths open while Billy and Finn told them what had happened. Wes and Jim seemed impressed, but Eddie looked doubtful.

"You found a crate of dynamite, and then it was just gone?" Eddie said. He kicked at the root of a fir tree. "You're fibbing."

"You're just jealous because we found the dynamite instead of you!" Finn said.

"Someone must have stolen it," Wes said.

"They could blow this place sky-high!" Jim added.

But Billy could see that Eddie still wasn't convinced.

"There aren't any folks like that in Scenic," Eddie said. "I bet there wasn't any dynamite, either." He turned and kept walking toward Lookout Rock. Wes and Jim followed him. "Nice try," Eddie scoffed over his shoulder.

"I know what we saw," Billy muttered to Finn. He slapped his brush into the jar of turpentine. "There must have been fifty sticks of dynamite in that crate."

Finn didn't answer right away. Then he said, "Listen, Billy. Your father told us to keep out of the shed. But...we can still look through the window, can't we?"

Billy caught on to his friend's idea. "Sure! We can look *outside* the shed all we want, too. Maybe we'll find something to help us figure out what happened to the dynamite!"

Leaving the jar and rags on the ground, the boys ran toward the shed. A piece of wood had been nailed across the door. Billy guessed his father had put it there after sending him and Finn home. The broken glass had been removed, too. A square of cardboard covered the hole, but Billy had no trouble prying it off.

"See anything?" Finn asked.

In the daylight, the shed didn't seem nearly as sinister as it had the night before. Billy looked around carefully. Once again he saw rolls of tarpaper, bins of nails, desks, chairs, and school supplies. Nothing looked any different.

"Guess my dad swept up all the dirt," he said. "Everything else looks like it was here already."

While Finn took his turn peering through the hole, Billy searched the ground outside the shed. "No footprints or anything," he mumbled. "Too many pine needles."

Just then, a flash of red among the branches caught his eye.

"Finn...look!" Billy called. He reached among the branches and pulled out a tattered piece of red plaid flannel. It was about two inches across, and frayed at the edges.

"Maybe whoever took that dynamite got his shirt caught on a branch!" Finn said. He took the scrap from Billy. "Do you think we can figure out where he went?"

"Well, we sure can try," Billy said.

The boys paced slowly around the shed. They walked in wider and wider circles, searching under rocks, among branches, and between tree roots. Squirrels, blue jays, and juncos objected noisily. But Billy and Finn didn't give up until it was time for supper.

"Nothing," Finn said with a sigh.

Billy shoved his hands into the pockets of his knickers. "How many people do you think live here?" he asked as they started toward home.

"In Scenic?" Finn shrugged. "Don't know. Hundreds, maybe. There must be forty or fifty bunkhouses, plus all the family cabins."

He and Billy climbed over a low hillside. The family cabins came into sight up ahead. The wood-sided buildings were tucked in among the fir trees next to the river. Billy spotted his own cabin, in front of the low bridge that crossed the Tye. His little sister, Marjorie, sat on the doorstep. She was playing with her doll.

"Out of all those men, I bet plenty have red-plaid shirts," said Billy.

"But not ripped ones," Finn said. "We'll have to keep our eyes open, that's all."

He scrambled down the other side of the hill.

"Knock-knock," he said, stopping suddenly.

"Who's there?" Billy said.

"Canoe," Finn said.

"Canoe who?" Billy said.

"Canoe tell me who the new girl is?" Finn asked.

Billy looked curiously toward the clearing.

Not many new families had arrived in Scenic lately. Most of the kids had come to the camp around the same time as Billy and Finn, when work on the tunnel first began.

Finn nodded at a small cabin on the far side of the

clearing. It had been boarded up all winter. Now the boards were gone and the windows were wide open. Just outside the front door, a girl was playing with a silky, red dog.

Billy guessed she was about the same age as him and Finn. She leaned forward, tempting the dog with a stick in her hand. The wind had blown her wavy, chin-length black hair around her face. Her skirt and sailor shirt were smudged with paw prints.

"Here, Buster." The girl held the stick just out of reach, laughing as the dog jumped for it. With a flick of her wrist, she sent the stick sailing across the clearing. "Go get it, boy!" she called. "Fetch!"

The stick landed in the dirt, right in front of Billy and Finn. Buster came bounding after it in a blur of scrambling paws and flying fur.

Billy got a look at the stick just as the dog's teeth closed around it. It was a perfect cylinder—with none of the funny bends and bumps pine branches usually had. Then he saw the stick's reddish color, and the powder that coated it.

A shiver ran down Billy's spine.

"That's no tree branch," he told Finn. "It's a stick of dynamite!"

CHAPTER FIVE

DANNIE

H ey!" Finn flew across the clearing, just as the girl pulled the stick from Buster's muzzle. "What are you trying to do?" he cried. "Get us all killed?"

The girl's dark eyes flashed. "Gee," she said. "It's nice to meet you, too."

Billy ran over to stand next to Finn.

"Don't you know what that is?" Billy asked the girl. "Dynamite! It could blow up any second!"

He pointed at the powdered cylinder. The girl looked at it uncertainly. "You mean this?" she asked, waving the stick in his face. "You're afraid of a dumb stick?"

"Didn't you hear me? It's *dynamite!*" Billy gasped. "Put that *down!*"

"You'd better tell us what you did with the rest of them, too," Finn said. "You're in a heap of trouble, stealing a whole crate of dynamite."

Bright red spots sprang to the girl's cheeks. She took a step back. It was as if Finn's words had pushed her.

"You think I... *stole* this thing?" she asked, still gripping the dynamite. "How can you say that? You don't even know me! Why, you mean, low-down little—"

At that moment, the door to the cabin swung open. A tall, thin man stepped into the doorway. His blue pants and gray shirt were faded and worn. His face was lean and sharp. There was a hard look in his eyes.

"Get inside, Dannie," he said gruffly.

Then the man saw the stick of dynamite in Dannie's hand. His eyes flickered nervously toward Billy and Finn. He came down the cabin steps and took the dynamite from her.

"Get inside now," he said again. "You and your brother still have unpacking to do."

Billy looked past the open door. A dark-haired, older boy stood inside. He was pulling tin plates and cups from a cardboard box on the floor. A bulb hung from the ceiling. It lit up a kitchen table piled high with pots, pans, and tins of food.

"Yes, Papa," Dannie said. She shot Finn and Billy a glare before climbing the three wooden steps to the door. Buster scrambled ahead of her.

Dannie's father strode to the edge of the river and

threw the dynamite into the water. The strong current quickly carried it out of sight. Dannie's father scowled when he saw that Billy and Finn were still standing there.

"You've got no business here," he said. "Now get lost, both of you."

He brushed past the boys and climbed the cabin steps in one long stride.

"Hey, mister! Wait!" Finn called. "Where did that dynamite—?"

Bang!

The door slammed shut.

"What was *that* all about?" Billy said in a low voice. "Dannie's father sure is ornery."

"Shhh!" Finn held a finger to his lips. He pointed to the open windows on either side of the door. Through them, the boys could hear a low, gruff voice.

"I don't want you two kids blabbing our business to anyone," Dannie's father was saying. "Understand? We don't need any trouble following us here from Chicago."

Finn poked Billy's arm. "Trouble?" he whispered. "What kind of trouble?"

Billy shrugged. "Don't know," he said.

Just then, he saw his mother step out of their cabin

and start across the clearing. In her hands was a steaming bowl of baked beans wrapped in a dishtowel. As usual, five-year-old Marjorie stuck to Mrs. Cole's side like her shadow.

Billy groaned. "Uh-oh. Why did she have to pick now to welcome Dannie's family to the camp?" he said.

"What if Dannie tells her we were asking about the dynamite?" Finn asked.

"Get ready for a lecture," Billy told his friend. "That's exactly what's in store for us if Mother finds out we disobeyed my dad."

"We'd better get out of here quick, then," Finn said. "At least we have a chance of getting supper at the cookhouse. And after that there's the Saturday picture at the recreation hall."

Billy knew he'd get in trouble later for skipping supper at home. But he and Finn couldn't just sit by and do nothing. Especially now that they had found the new girl in camp with that stick of dynamite.

"What are we waiting for?" he said. "Let's go!"

* * *

Billy and Finn crossed the river and followed the road toward the main part of Scenic. When they reached the lodge, they climbed up onto the walkways. Workers were just coming off the last shift. Most of them were headed toward the cookhouse. Their loud voices echoed in the air.

"I don't trust that Dannie girl," Finn said. "Or her dad. Did you see how quick he got her away from us? I just know he's hiding something."

Billy shoved his hands in the pockets of his knickers. "You know what kind of trouble they have in Chicago?" he said. "Gangsters! I hear Mother and Dad talking about it sometimes. Al Capone and his mob are shooting up the whole city to get control of the bootleg liquor business."

Billy knew that a law had been passed to make it illegal for anyone to sell or drink liquor in the U.S. That was why there was no alcohol allowed in the Scenic camp—even though some of the men complained bitterly.

"You think Dannie's father was a gangster in Chicago?" Finn asked excitedly.

Billy's own mind started to fill with pictures of men in fancy suits, with guns and shiny black cars. It was hard to imagine such things in quiet, peaceful Scenic. "Maybe gangsters want to do business here," he said with a shrug.

Up ahead, a crowd of men waited on the platform

outside the cookhouse. Their work pants, jackets, and coveralls were stained with sweat, grease, and granite dust. As Billy and Finn got closer, Chef Whitman opened the doors and the men crowded in.

"Well, we saw that crate yesterday," Finn said. "And Dannie and her family just got here."

Billy thought about that as he and Finn stepped through the doors. A few of the men looked at them when they took their places in line. Children were supposed to eat in their cabins. But Chef Whitman had never turned Billy or Finn away. The jolly, round man was in charge of the crew of men who kept the cookhouse running around the clock.

Billy spotted their friend right away, standing next to an enormous vat on one of the stoves. His chef's hat was tilted back on his balding head. His white apron barely covered his middle. When he saw Billy and Finn, Chef Whitman raised a bushy eyebrow and winked.

Billy breathed in the smells of beef, bread, and potatoes. His mouth was watering already. "I bet Al Capone's men wouldn't think twice about stealing a crate of dynamite," he said. "Or even blowing up the whole camp!"

Finn reached into his pocket and pulled out the scrap of red plaid flannel. "We'd better find out quick if Dannie's father has a shirt like this," he said. "If he's hiding the rest of that dynamite somewhere—"

"What's this about dynamite?" a deep, gravely voice spoke up behind Billy and Finn.

Billy had been so busy thinking about Al Capone and Dannie's father that he'd forgotten there were other people around. But when he saw the weathered, wrinkled face that looked down at him and Finn, he wasn't worried.

"Hey, Mr. Pratt," he said.

The way Billy saw it, Gus Pratt had to be one of the oldest men at the Scenic camp. Maybe even the oldest man in Washington State. His hair was silver-white, and he had a stooped, grizzled look that hinted at years of hard work. But the expression in Gus's blue eyes was sharp. He still worked the night shift on one of the powder crews. During his off hours, he sometimes fished with Billy and Finn, or joked with them at the Saturday moving picture. "Being around you boys is good medicine for an old coot like me," Gus always told them.

"Don't tell me you scrappers have been fool enough to mess with explosives," Gus said, shaking a finger. He glanced at the scrap of fabric in Finn's hand, then reached for a plate from the scarred serving table.

"No, sir," Finn promised. "Not on purpose, any-how. But guess what we found in the—"

Just then, a stocky, barrel-chested young man elbowed Gus into the boys. The man's denim pants and work shirt were clean, as if he hadn't yet begun his shift. His reddish face was framed by thick black hair.

"Move aside, you crazy geezer," the young man barked. "I haven't got all day." He stepped right in front of Gus and grabbed a plate.

Gus frowned. "Now look here, Frank Dempsey," he said. "You can't do that."

"Oh, yeah?" Frank held out his plate so that Chef Whitman could spoon stew onto it. Then he strode over to one of the long dining tables and sat down.

"Don't let him treat you like that, Mr. Pratt!" Billy whispered.

"Frank Dempsey! You in here?" Another man's voice rose above the noisy clatter of plates and chairs and knives and forks.

Billy knew that voice. "Your father!" he whispered to Finn.

Finn had already ducked behind Gus Pratt. Billy stepped back, too. Finn's father took a few steps into the cookhouse, limping on his left leg. He held a clip-board under his arm.

"Dempsey!" he called again.

"Over here." Frank stood up and marched over to Finn's father. "Matter of fact, I wanted to see *you,* Mr. Mackenzie. I was hoping to get an advance on my pay."

Gus shook his head in disgust. "That mealy-mouthed bully can't even make it to payday," he muttered to the boys.

Billy was just glad that Finn's father wasn't looking for him and Finn. Not now, anyway. Billy reached for a plate while Mr. Mackenzie and Frank spoke in low tones.

All of a sudden, Frank's voice began to rise. "How should I know if there's a crate of dynamite missing?" he sputtered. "You're the supervisor. Seems to me you ought to know how much dynamite we've got. If you're doing your job right, that is."

Next to Billy, Finn's whole body went stiff. "He's trying to make my dad look bad!" Finn whispered angrily.

"Right now my job is to account for all the dynamite here in camp," Mr. Mackenzie said. He flipped through the wrinkled papers on his clipboard. "These records show that you signed for a crate of dynamite yesterday. The shift foreman tells me it was never used in the tunnel. I need to know what you did with it, Frank."

Finn and Billy stared at each other. A crate of dynamite was missing! Could Frank be the one who had taken it?

"I never signed for any dynamite," Frank insisted.

The cookhouse had gone silent.

Finn's father jabbed a finger at one of the papers. "Your name's right here on the sheet," he said. "Frank Dempsey. That *is* your name, isn't it, son?"

Frank swatted Mr. Mackenzie's hand away. "Are you calling me a liar?" he said. He turned away slightly and drew back his arm.

Finn moved like lightning. He ran over and wedged himself between his father and Frank Dempsey. He shoved at Frank's chest with both hands, trying to push the angry man back.

"Look out, Finn!" Billy cried.

But it was too late. Frank Dempsey's fist was shooting straight toward his friend!

Chapter Six

FLYING FISTS

No!" Billy shouted to his friend.

But Frank Dempsey's punch was coming, sure as the Northern Express.

Somehow Finn got his elbow up. Frank's fist missed Finn's cheek and glanced off the top of his head.

"Huh?" Frank stumbled backward, blinking. "Who's this kid?"

"Take back what you said about my dad!" Finn shouted. *"You're* the one who's up to no good!"

He lunged toward Frank.

"That's enough!" Mr. Mackenzie grabbed Finn by the shoulder and hauled him over to where Billy stood. "You boys shouldn't even be in here. You know that," he said.

"Yes, sir." Billy said. He glanced at Frank. The stocky man stood in the doorway, glaring at Finn's father. Billy lowered his voice. "Sir, do you think Mr. Dempsey took that dynamite?" he asked.

Finn's father looked long and hard at Billy. "We still don't know for sure that any dynamite is missing," he said. "Your father and I are looking into the matter, Billy. And we don't want you boys interfering."

"But Dad!" Finn said. "There's a new family in camp. We saw the girl with—"

"No buts about it," Mr. Mackenzie said. "I want you two out of here. This instant!"

Billy saw the frustration on Finn's face. He felt the same way. But what could they do?

* * *

"Knock-knock," Billy said, as soon as he and Finn were outside of the cookhouse.

Finn's frown lightened. "Who's there?" he asked.

"Midas," Billy told him.

"Midas who?"

"Midas well go to the picture show," said Billy. "We can look for someone wearing a red plaid shirt with a piece ripped out of it."

Finn nodded. "We can't just wait around for our dads to figure out the dynamite's missing. It's up to us to do something about it!" he said. "Maybe Mr. Dempsey will go to the picture, too. Then we can keep an eye on him. And on that girl, Dannie."

"I bet she won't come. Her father doesn't want her mixing with folks here, remember?" Billy said.

The recreation hall was the heart and soul of the Scenic camp. That was what Billy's mother always said. It was the place where men played basketball, checkers, or cards when they weren't on shift. Every kind of social event was held there—dances, plays, church services, and even meetings of the Scenic Ladies Society. Twice every week, on Tuesdays and Saturdays, people made their way to the hall from all over camp for Billy's favorite event—the moving picture show.

The sun had just gone down. Billy and Finn walked to the recreation hall and stepped up to the ticket booth. The women in the Scenic Ladies Society usually took turns taking money. Tonight Lucy's mother, Mrs. Grinnell, sat behind the cash box. Tacked to the front of the booth was a piece of cardboard with the title of the movie printed on it: *The Gold Rush.*

"Why, hello, boys," Mrs. Grinnell said. "I see you're in plenty of time for Charlie Chaplin's latest picture."

"Yes, ma'am," Finn said.

Billy fished for a dime in his pocket and gazed into

the main room. Most of the chairs were still empty. They would fill up once the men finished their suppers. Mr. Farnam was on the stage, using a long pole to unroll the screen from the ceiling. Wes and a few other kids darted around in front of the stage. Billy and Finn went over to join them.

"Well, look who showed up," a smug voice said.

It was Alice Ann. She and Lucy sat at the piano next to the stage. Both girls wore pleated skirts and sweaters buttoned over their blouses. They passed a bag of cookies between them.

"We always come to the Saturday picture," Billy said. Seeing the bag of cookies made his stomach start growling as loudly as the motor of the Model T automobile his father kept near their cabin.

"I figured you two might be busy looking for D-Y-N-A-M-I-T-E," Alice Ann said. She crossed one ankle neatly over the other. "You know, that no one saw except you?"

Billy got a funny feeling. Had everyone in Scenic heard that story by now? Were they all laughing at him and Finn? Billy scowled at Wes, who suddenly seemed very interested in a bug crawling on the floor. "Blabbermouth," he muttered.

"Just 'cause no one else saw it doesn't mean it wasn't there," Finn said.

"We don't believe that for a second," said Alice Ann. She passed the bag of cookies to Lucy. "Isn't that right?"

Lucy nodded. Not that Billy expected her to do anything else. She always followed Alice Ann's lead. Billy was so annoyed with both of them that he reached out and snatched the bag of cookies from Lucy.

"You give that back!" she said.

Billy tossed the bag over her head to Finn.

"Ha!" Finn waved the bag at Alice Ann to tease her. She leaped off the piano bench and ran toward him. Finn threw the bag back to Billy.

"Billy, over here!" Wes called, joining the game.

"Hey, now! None of that, boys," Mr. Farnam called. But he was too busy with the screen to do much more than scold.

The boys ran circles around Alice Ann and Lucy. At last the girls gave up.

Finn, Billy, and Wes ran laughing behind the stage curtain and began cramming cookies into their mouths.

Billy was so hungry that he didn't say a word until the last crumb was gone. Then he turned to Wes and said, "So how many people did you blab to, Wes Gundy?"

"Alice Ann and Lucy, that's all." Wes scrunched the empty bag into a tight wad. "So what did you do with that dynamite?"

"It's a secret," Finn told him. "And *you* can't keep one. Anyhow, we're busy. Me and Billy have important work to do." He pulled the scrap of red plaid fabric from his pocket.

"Important *secret* work," Billy added. "So don't bug us, Wes." He peeked around the curtain, looking carefully at the people who were taking their seats.

"What are you looking for?" Wes asked. He looked through the curtains, too. "Uh-oh. Here comes Miss Wrigley!"

The chairs had been arranged with an aisle down the center. Their teacher walked briskly down it, staring straight at the gap in the curtain where Billy, Finn, and Wes stood.

She wasn't smiling.

"Boys!" Miss Wrigley called. "Is it true that you took an entire bag of cookies from Alice Ann and Lucy?"

The two girls were sitting in the front row of chairs. Billy made a face at them. Then he saw another girl enter the hall.

"Finn, look!" he said. "It's Dannie!"

Miss Wrigley whirled in the direction of the door. "Oh, my!" she said. "I do so want to meet Daniella. Alice Ann, Lucy, would you please come with me? I'm sure Daniella will want to make new friends here in Scenic."

42

Miss Wrigley and the two girls made a beeline for Dannie. They reached her just as her father and brother finished at the ticket booth and joined her. Billy couldn't hear what Miss Wrigley was saying. But she seemed to be bubbling over with enthusiasm.

"Dannie's family will have a tough time keeping to themselves with Miss Wrigley around," Finn said.

Dannie shifted nervously from foot to foot while Miss Wrigley babbled on. She glanced at Alice Ann and Lucy, and Billy thought he saw her frown. Dannie's father didn't crack a single smile as Miss Wrigley pumped his hand. He looked uneasy, as if he wanted to pull free and run from the recreation hall.

"If they don't want to talk to folks, why'd they come to the picture in the first place?" Billy said.

"Beats me," said Finn. He jumped down from the stage. "Come on. Let's go hear what they're saying."

The recreation hall was filling up fast. Wes took a seat close to the screen, but Billy and Finn headed for the empty chairs in the last row, close to Miss Wrigley and Dannie's family.

"...I'm so looking forward to having Daniella in my class," Miss Wrigley was saying. She glanced toward the entrance. "Will Mrs. Renwick be joining you for the picture this evening?" she asked.

A pained look flashed across Mr. Renwick's face.

"It's just Dannie and Mike and me," he said gruffly. "My wife passed away."

"Oh, my. I'm so sorry to hear it," Miss Wrigley said quickly. "Rest assured that I will do all I can to provide a proper womanly influence for Daniella, Mr. Renwick."

"Dannie's in for it now," Finn mumbled to Billy.

"Daniella, I'd like you to meet two of the girls in your class," Miss Wrigley went on. "This is—"

"I'm doing just fine," Dannie said bluntly. "And everyone calls me Dannie, not Daniella."

"Oh," said Miss Wrigley. Even without turning around, Billy could tell the teacher was frowning. "I see."

"I'm Alice Ann, and this is Lucy," Alice Ann spoke up. "Do you like to sew? Lucy and I are embroidering handkerchiefs."

"Sew?" Dannie gave a loud snort. "I'd rather be thrown into a pit of rattlesnakes!"

Billy tried not to laugh. When he looked over his shoulder again, it seemed like he was watching two armies face off with each other. On one side were Alice Ann, Lucy, and Miss Wrigley. They were armed with their neat skirts and sweaters and their sweet smiles. On the other side were Dannie and her father and brother, with their angry glares and their faded clothes.

Just then, Mr. Farnam stepped over to the group.

"We can start any time you're ready," he told Miss Wrigley. "The projector is all set up."

Billy didn't miss the funny tone in Mr. Farnam's voice. Or the way several men lifted their hats to say, "Evening, Miss Wrigley," as they passed. But if Miss Wrigley was sweet on any of them, she didn't let on. She hurried to the piano at the front of the room, ready to play music for whatever mood the picture needed: happy, sad, funny, or exciting.

Billy kept an eye on the Renwicks. They took seats two rows ahead. Moments later, the lights went off and the picture began. Miss Wrigley's jaunty piano playing filled the recreation hall. Billy laughed as Charlie Chaplin moved along the snowy cliffs of Alaska in his funny penguin walk. He forgot all about the missing dynamite—until he felt Finn's elbow jab him in the side.

"Look, Mr. Renwick's leaving," Finn whispered. "The picture's hardly started."

Billy squinted into the darkened room until he spotted Mr. Renwick's tall silhouette. Sure enough, Dannie's father was striding quickly toward the door.

"Let's find out where he's going," Billy whispered.

The two boys got up from their seats and hurried outside. Billy blinked in the harsh glare from the lightbulb above the door. He and Finn escaped from the recreation hall as quickly as they could, jumping down off the walkway and into the shadows. The pine needles were so thick that the boys barely made a sound as they landed.

They crouched in the darkness, listening. The faint pounding of drills echoed from the tunnel entrance. Much closer, Billy heard the *thump-thump-thump* of Mr. Renwick's shoes on the walkway.

"Sounds like he's heading toward the lodge," Finn whispered.

Billy leaned out a bit, just far enough to see Dannie's father. Mr. Renwick looked like a tall black streak against the dark gray night. Silently, Billy and Finn followed him. Billy turned to look behind them.

"Did you hear that?" he asked Finn.

Finn shook his head. "Hear what?"

Billy didn't know for sure. Drilling from the tunnel still hummed in the background. But there was something else, too. A rustling noise. Billy stared into the blackness but saw nothing. "Nothing, I guess," he whispered.

Ahead of them, Mr. Renwick's footsteps stopped at the lodge. Dannie's father bent close to a door at the side of the building. The windows on either side of the door were dark. A sign above the door gleamed in the moonlight: SECURITY OFFICE.

"What's he up to?" Billy whispered.

He and Finn heard muttering sounds. Then the rattle of a doorknob.

"He's trying to bust in!" Finn cried.

Billy put a finger to his lips. But it was too late. Finn had spoken too loudly. Dannie's father sprang away from the door. He shot a startled glance in the boys' direction. Then he jumped down from the walkway. He bolted toward the trees behind the lodge. Seconds later, he seemed to melt into the shadows.

"Come on!" Billy told Finn.

The two boys broke into a run. When they reached the trees, Billy felt a cold blanket of pine-scented air wrap around him. He saw the glowing eyes of an owl, and heard creatures scuttling away. The fir trees looked like sinister cloaked figures about to reach out and grab him. As Billy ran, he heard it again—the rustling noise behind them.

Swish, swish…

"Finn!" Billy's voice came out in a high squeak.

He still didn't know who—or what—was making that sound. But he didn't want to be anywhere near it.

He raced after Finn, stumbling over roots and tugging his shirt loose from branches. He heard splashing up ahead, and then he and Finn waded across the Tye. Billy's feet were sopping wet inside his boots when he and Finn reached the clearing next to the school-house.

"Up there!" Finn said, pointing above Lookout Rock.

At first, all Billy saw was the silvery glow of the moon over the mountainside. Then he spotted something else farther down—the yellow beam of a flashlight. It flick-ered among the trees just above Lookout Rock. Billy frowned as he watched the light move slowly up the mountain.

"What's Mr. Renwick going up there for?"

"There's only one way to find out." Finn started up the path to Lookout Rock. "Are you coming?" he called over his shoulder.

"Are you crazy?" Billy said. "There are mountain lions up there. Grizzlies! Or what if we slip and get hurt, or..."

He didn't even want to think about what might hap-pen if they caught up to Mr. Renwick. Or what their parents would do if they found out he and Finn had climbed up the mountain on their own at night.

Finn scrambled to keep his footing on the steep

slope. "Maybe Mr. Renwick hid that crate of dynamite up there. Maybe he'll come back and blow up the whole town."

"Okay, okay!"

Somehow, Billy made himself climb to the top of Lookout Rock. The hairs stood up on the back of his neck as he and Finn made their way past the shadows of their cannon and fort. Above them, the flashlight flickered in and out of sight.

Billy stumbled along the path. Every rustle and squeak made him jump.

"Hear that?" Finn asked.

Billy heard it, all right. A shuffling noise too loud for a porcupine or wood vole. "Footsteps!" he hissed.

It sounded as if Mr. Renwick was just up the slope from him and Finn. Yet when Billy peered up at the dark snarl of trees, he saw no flashlight beam.

"I don't get it," he muttered. "Where did he go?"

A deep grunt echoed in the darkness. Billy heard dirt and pebbles rain down the hillside toward him and Finn. In the next instant, a series of crashing thumps shook the ground under Billy's feet.

He stared up the mountain—then gasped. A huge ball of rock was heading straight for them!

"A boulder!" Billy cried. "Run!"

CHAPTER SEVEN

TOO CLOSE

Finn slammed into Billy's side, knocking the breath right out of him. They both went flying from the path.

Billy tumbled head over heels in an avalanche of dirt and rocks. The whole mountain seemed to be crashing down around him.

Bam!

The boulder banged into the ground right next to Billy. He felt as if a stick of dynamite had exploded inside his head. A shower of pebbles rained down on him. Then the boulder tumbled past, thudding down the mountainside.

"Ooomph!" Billy crashed into a thick wall of prickly pine branches. Gasping for air, he managed to raise his head. He had fallen all the way back down to their fort.

"Finn?" Billy called. *"Finn!"*

A stirring of branches came from the other side of the fort. "R-right here," Finn said. He shuddered as he stood up slowly and brushed pine needles from his shirt and knickers. "That sure was close."

Billy gazed up the mountainside, looking for Mr. Renwick's flashlight beam. "Dannie's father pushed that boulder at us on purpose!" he said.

He didn't see or hear anything moving above them. But suddenly he heard thumping footsteps below Lookout Rock. "Huh?" he murmured.

"Someone's there!" Finn whispered. "Someone else."

"So somebody was following us," Billy said. "And he's running away. Let's get him!"

Billy had never moved so fast down the steep path. There were bruises and scratches up and down his arms and legs, but he ignored them. By the time he and Finn reached the bottom, the footsteps had faded away. All the boys heard was the babbling river.

Then Billy spotted a powerful beam cutting through the darkness. The light was coming from the direction of the family cabins. "Finn, look!" he cried, pointing. "He's coming back!"

Finn's mouth dropped open as the person came closer. "It's Mr. Jenkins," he said.

Mr. Jenkins was the chief of security at Scenic. The beam lit his red face and bulging belly. "What in the world are you boys doing out here?" he called. "You scared me half to death with all that crashing and yelling!"

"We were following Mr. Renwick," Billy told him. "He tried to kill us...with that!"

He pointed at the boulder. The huge piece of rock had hit a fir tree close to Lookout Rock. It stood almost as high as Billy's waist. The boulder had struck with such force that the tree was tilted. Half its roots had pulled loose from the ground.

Mr. Jenkins frowned. Then he shined his beam up the mountainside. "There's no one up there," he said. "Are you sure you saw someone?"

"Yes, sir," Finn said. "There was another person, too. Down here. You didn't see anyone?"

"No," Mr. Jenkins answered. He raised an eyebrow. "Just how many folks do you think are out to get you boys?"

It sounded as if the security chief was teasing them. "Mr. Jenkins, this is serious!" Billy said. "What if Mr. Renwick's planning to do something with the missing dynamite?"

"Al Capone's mob could blow this whole camp sky high!" Finn added.

"Al Capone?" Mr. Jenkins chuckled. "Whatever gave you boys an idea like that?"

Billy stared at the ground. Finn kicked at a pebble. First Eddie and Wes and their dads and everyone else didn't believe them. Now Mr. Jenkins was laughing at them, too.

"Boulders do sometimes fall down the mountainside on their own," Mr. Jenkins went on. "That's why it's so dangerous up here. I'll tell you what. I'll climb up and take a look. I might even decide to keep this just between us. I see no reason to worry your parents, since no one got hurt."

Well, that was one good thing, Billy told himself.

"But," Mr. Jenkins added, "you have to promise me something." He gave Finn and Billy a look that was all business. "Forget about looking for any dynamite. From now on, I want you boys to mind your own business."

With that, Mr. Jenkins sent them home.

"Why are people always telling us that?" Billy grumbled, as he and Finn walked toward the family cabins.

Finn glanced back at Mr. Jenkins's flashlight beam moving up the mountainside. "I wonder where Mr. Renwick is now?" he said. "He has to be up to no good. If he wasn't, he never would have—"

Boom!

A deafening explosion made both boys jump half a foot in the air.

"Dynamite!" Billy breathed.

An explosion that loud couldn't have come from inside the tunnel.

Someone had set off explosives right in the camp!

CHAPTER EIGHT

KA-BOOM!

Come on!" Finn yelled, yanking on Billy's sleeve. The boys raced back to Lookout Rock. By the time they reached the top of the ledge, Billy's heart was pounding with fear. He looked out over the camp and gasped.

"Jeepers!" he exclaimed.

A huge ball of flame lit the night sky. Fire shot up and over the bunkhouses. It bathed their roofs in an eerie, flickering orange glow.

"Billy! Finn!" Mr. Jenkins called from up the mountainside. His flashlight beam wagged wildly as he ran toward them. His round face was tight with worry. "Go to your father's office, Billy," he said, puffing. "Get the Skykomish police on the phone. Tell them to send the fire brigade right away!"

Then he skidded out of sight down the side of Lookout Rock.

Billy and Finn didn't have to be told twice. They climbed back down from the rock and raced across camp. As they passed behind the family cabins, doors opened. People ran outside, calling to one another in alarm. But Billy and Finn didn't stop. They rushed past to the road and ran breathlessly to the old lodge.

Mr. Cole had one of the few telephones in all of Scenic. Billy had never used it before, but he had seen his father make calls. As soon as he and Finn burst into the office, Billy made a leap for the desk. Papers went flying as he grabbed the handset and jiggled the receiver. It seemed like forever before the operator came on the line.

"Connect me to the Skykomish police, please," Billy shouted into the mouthpiece. "Right away!"

"Young man," the operator said. "Do your mother and father know you're using the telephone?"

"There's a fire!" Billy said. "Mr. Jenkins told me to call. We need fire trucks up at the Scenic camp!"

"A fire?" The operator sounded worried now. "Was there an accident in the tunnel?"

Billy nearly leaped out of his skin in frustration. "Yes. I mean, no! Not in the tunnel," he said. "Just put me through...*please!*"

"There's no need to be rude, young man," the operator said. "What did you say your name was?"

Billy sighed. "I didn't. But it's Billy. Billy Cole."

"Why, you must be James Cole's son!" the operator cooed. "My husband tells me he's the general manager up there at Scenic...."

Finn shook his head. "Oh, brother!" he whispered.

The operator fired half a dozen more questions at Billy before she finally put through the call. "You tell the folks up there at Scenic that Ida Hawkins is always ready to help in an emergency," she said. "Please hold for the Skykomish police...."

* * *

Billy's eyes stung as he and Finn ran from his father's office toward the flames. A thick cloud of smoke had settled over the bunkhouses. Through it, Billy could make out dozens of men stumbling from the buildings. Noise came from everywhere: shouting, blasting car horns, and the terrified, high-pitched neighing of horses.

The hot air held a distinctive odor that Billy recognized at once.

"Dynamite!" he said. "I knew it!"

Flashlight beams cut through the smoky night. People ran along the walkways and the road, carrying shovels and bandages and blankets.

"Is it the bunkhouses?" Billy heard Mrs. Lockhart ask. "Is anyone hurt?"

Billy squinted into the thick smoke. Flames still jumped high into the air, but they seemed to be coming from behind the bunkhouses. Billy and Finn squeezed through the crowd, moving closer to the crackling heat.

"Billy, look!" Finn said. "The garage is blown out!"

A huge, barn-like garage stood just beyond the bunkhouses. Cars, horses, and machines were kept there. An entire wall of the building was missing and flames were leaping through the roof. Men were leading horses out, but terrified neighing could still be heard from inside.

"Cripes!" Billy looked at the bunkhouse closest to the garage. A chill wind blew sparks straight toward the building. "The fire could spread to the bunkhouses!"

Mr. Mackenzie and Billy's father seemed worried about that, too. Billy saw them struggle to control a powerful jet of water that sprayed from a thick hose. They aimed it at the bunkhouse wall, soaking it thoroughly before turning the hose back to the fire.

"The Skykomish fire brigade better get here quick," Finn said. "That hose is hardly slowing down the flames at all."

Gus Pratt was leading a black mare through the garage doors amid a choking cloud of smoke. The horse reared up. Her nostrils flared and her eyes were wide with panic. As Gus pulled on the reins, he coughed into a bandanna tied over his mouth.

"He needs water," Billy said. He nodded at the sweaty, red-faced men who were racing past Gus to get machinery and cars from inside the garage. "They all do!"

"We can get some from the cookhouse," Finn said.

As he and Finn spun away from the fire, Billy saw Wes, Eddie, and Jim standing near the bunkhouses. Next to them, Alice Ann, Janet, and Lucy helped their mothers tend to a handful of men who sat hunched over and coughing nearby. Billy looked for his own mother until Janet said, "She's not here, Billy. She stayed behind to look after Marjorie and some of the other little ones."

"Looks like you were right about that missing dynamite," Jim said.

"Someone blew out the garage on purpose!" Wes added.

Eddie stood silently by. He sure wasn't making fun of him and Finn now, Billy noticed. But that didn't make Billy feel any better. Not when roaring flames were swallowing more of the garage every second.

"Do they know who did it?" Finn asked.

Wes shook his head. "Not yet."

They didn't have time to stand around and make guesses. Within minutes, Billy and Finn were lugging a heavy bucket of water between them. They circled around one side of the garage. Wes and Eddie carried a second bucket the other way.

"Want a drink, Dad?" Billy asked. He and Finn set their bucket down in front of the men who held the fire hose.

Mr. Cole's face was red and smudged with soot. He barely took his eyes off the flames as he gulped from the tin cup and wiped his mouth with his sleeve.

"Thanks, boys." He dipped the cup in the bucket again and handed it to Mr. Mackenzie. "That sure hits the spot."

Just then, Frank Dempsey stepped down off the walkway from the bunkhouses. He didn't look hot and sweaty, like the men who were fighting the fire. He carried a shovel. Dirt was caked on it, and on his boots.

"Where's *he* been that he was too busy to help out here?" Billy said.

Mr. Cole frowned, keeping a tight grip on the hose. "Didn't I make myself clear yesterday? You boys are to mind your own affairs," he said firmly.

"Yes, Dad," Billy said. He sighed and picked up the

water bucket. But Finn didn't move. He stared beyond Frank Dempsey.

"Look who *else* just got here," Finn murmured.

Dannie's father was pushing his way through the crowd toward the fire. Dannie, her big brother Mike, and Buster stayed behind. As Mr. Renwick passed Billy and Finn, he fixed them with a cold glare. Billy took a step back.

"Should we go get Mr. Jenkins?" he whispered to Finn. "Mr. Renwick already tried to kill us. What's he up to now?"

"I bet he *is* a gangster!" Finn said, scowling. "He probably set off this blast."

He clamped his mouth shut as Dannie Renwick walked up to them. Buster danced from paw to paw beside her, sniffing the hot, smoky air.

"You boys sure are busy tonight," Dannie said.

"Everyone's busy," Finn said. "A building blew up. Didn't you notice?"

"Oh, I noticed, all right," Dannie said. "I notice a *lot* more than you two might think." There was a challenge in her eyes.

"What's *that* supposed to mean?" Billy demanded.

Dannie shrugged. Then she turned and walked away. Billy started after her.

"Aw, forget about her," Finn said. "Who cares what she says?"

Just then, sirens began to wail in the distance. "The trucks from Skykomish!" Billy said. "Took them long enough."

Two fire trucks roared along the road with their lights flashing. Suddenly, people were everywhere, amid a tangle of hoses. Calls for water kept Billy and Finn so busy that they didn't have a second to think about anything else. By the time the fire was finally under control, long past midnight, Billy's arms ached from lugging the heavy pail. He was so tired he could barely keep his eyes open. He and Finn walked back to their cabins with slow, dragging feet.

"Billy!" His mother jumped up from the kitchen table the moment he opened the door. She hurried past little Evie Kleig and her baby brother Hank, who slept wrapped in blankets on the rug in the front room.

"Thank goodness you're all right!" she said, burying Billy in a big hug.

"The fire's under control," he said, following his mother to the kitchen. The smell of baked beans made his stomach growl. "They stopped it before it spread to the bunkhouses. No one got hurt."

"Well, that's a blessing," his mother said. "But I was

talking about something else." She took a plateful of beans and bread from the oven and set it on the table. "What is this I hear about you and Finn leaving the picture show and going off by yourselves tonight? Onto the mountain, no less? Have you lost all good sense?"

Billy froze with his hand on his fork. He'd been so caught up in the excitement of the fire that he'd forgotten all about following Mr. Renwick. And hadn't Mr. Jenkins promised not to say anything to their parents?

"You're just lucky people here look out for one another," his mother went on. "That nice new girl Dannie Renwick came by to tell me she saw you two up above Lookout Rock. She was worried sick you might be attacked by a grizzly."

Billy jolted straight up in his chair. "Dannie?" he said.

So *she* was the person he had heard behind him and Finn on the mountain! While they were following her father, she had followed *them*!

Billy's mother continued to scold, but Billy wasn't listening.

Worried sick? Ha! Dannie sure hadn't acted very worried when she saw him and Finn at the fire. She'd just wanted to get him in hot water! Billy was willing to bet Dannie had gone to Finn's mother with the same story. And he knew why.

Those Renwicks have the dynamite, Billy told himself. *And they want to make sure Finn and I don't find it!*

He gulped, remembering the explosion in the garage. Tonight's horror had left a dark cloud over the whole town of Scenic.

What would be next? he wondered with a sick feeling in his stomach.

The trouble in camp was just beginning.

CHAPTER NINE

A TRAIL OF CLUES

Smoke still hung over Scenic the next morning. As Billy sat through Reverend Silsby's Sunday service, he saw more than a few bleary eyes. Even Alice Ann, sitting in the front row with her mother and older sister, yawned a few times.

Marjorie was one of the few people who was wide awake. She twisted and squirmed in the chair next to Billy's, flipping through the pages of her prayer book.

"Where are we up to now, Billy?" she whispered, for the hundredth time.

Billy found the page for her, then tugged at the tie his mother had made him wear. He couldn't stop thinking that a dynamite thief was loose, up to who-knew-what. And no one else was doing a thing about it!

He shot a frustrated glance at his parents. They were calmly listening to the sermon. In front of him, Finn sat sandwiched between his mother and father. His unruly hair had been slicked down. Billy didn't dare tap him on the shoulder. Still, he noticed that the sermon didn't stop his father from leaning forward to speak to Mr. Mackenzie.

"I talked to the afternoon watchman myself," Finn's father was saying, in a hushed whisper. "He only left the storage shed for a minute, to check on some noise outside. When he came back, a crate of dynamite had been signed out. By Frank Dempsey."

Billy sat up straighter.

"But Frank works the graveyard shift," Billy's father whispered back. "The dynamite was signed for at three o'clock Friday afternoon."

Billy's mother touched Mr. Cole's arm and raised an eyebrow. Billy's father sat back and looked at Reverend Silsby again.

Billy tapped his boot impatiently on the floor. He couldn't stop thinking about what he'd just heard. His father had said that Frank worked the graveyard shift. That was from midnight to eight in the morning. Frank shouldn't have been anywhere near any dynamite at three in the afternoon.

Billy wondered about something else, too. Why had Frank bothered to sign for the dynamite at all? With the guard gone, he could have just taken it.

Finn turned his head slightly. "Knock-knock," he whispered.

"Who's there?" Billy whispered back.

"Wyatt," said Finn.

"Wyatt who?" Billy asked.

"Wyatt do you think Dannie and her family aren't here?" he said.

"Shhhh!" Billy's mother frowned at the boys.

Finn turned quickly away. But Billy thought about what his friend had said. Why *wasn't* Dannie's family here?

Billy knew the Sunday service wasn't for everyone. Plenty of men were on shift inside the tunnel. Others simply didn't care to attend. Mr. Renwick had made it clear that he wanted his family to keep to themselves. Billy wished he knew why.

The windows of the recreation hall were open. As Billy listened to the faint thumping of drills and air pumps from the tunnel, his mind swirled. Whoever had taken the crate of explosives wasn't afraid to use it. And he and Finn had seen Dannie with a stick of dynamite. But if the Renwicks *were* bringing gangster trouble to Scenic, why had Frank Dempsey signed for the missing dynamite? Did Mr. Dempsey and Dannie's family know each other?

"So why'd you do it, old man?" A voice outside the window interrupted Billy's thoughts.

The voice wasn't very loud, but there was something familiar about it. No one else seemed to have heard it. Billy leaned across Marjorie to look out the window.

Frank Dempsey was blocking the path of a smaller man Billy couldn't see. Then Frank turned slightly, and Billy recognized Gus Pratt's wrinkled face. The old man carried his fishing pole. His worn, leather tackle bag was slung over his shoulder.

Gus said something Billy couldn't hear. He tried to step past, but Frank blocked his way. "Touch my things again, and you'll be sorry," Frank said, jabbing a finger at Gus's chest.

This time, Finn heard the voices too. He whipped his head around toward the window.

At that moment Miss Wrigley began pounding out the chords of a hymn on the piano. Everyone stood, and the boys' view of Frank and Gus was blocked. Finn shot a baffled glance over his shoulder at Billy. When at last the service was over, the boys hurried outside ahead of their parents.

"They're gone," Billy said, looking up and down the walkway.

"Who's gone, Billy?" Marjorie asked, appearing at his elbow.

Billy didn't answer her. "Mr. Pratt looked like he was going fishing," he said to Finn. "Maybe we can catch up to him and find out what he and Mr. Dempsey were arguing about."

"Wait a minute." Finn pointed up the mountain. "Look! Near Lookout Rock."

Lookout Rock was halfway across the camp, but Billy saw a dark-haired girl above the rocky ledge. Something else was moving up there, too. A dog.

"Dannie and Buster!" he said. "Let's go after them."

"I'm coming, too!" Marjorie said. She grabbed Billy's shirt.

Billy pulled away. "Not now, Marjorie," he said impatiently.

"Yes! NOW!" Marjorie wailed. She stomped her foot, and half a dozen people turned to stare. "Mother and Daddy said you're to look after me today. All day. *That'll* keep you from climbing up the mountain after nightfall, young man."

His sister had done a perfect imitation of their mother. But Billy didn't laugh.

"We can't bring her," Finn said. "We'll never catch up!"

Marjorie's lower lip started to tremble. Billy glanced at his parents, who stood talking to Reverend Silsby just outside the door of the recreation hall. If he disobeyed them, he'd be in worse trouble than ever. But they couldn't let Dannie get away. She was already disappearing among the trees across camp.

Then Billy spotted Alice Ann and Lucy. The girls were leaving the service together. Billy saw Alice Ann pull some colored thread and a crisp square of cotton cloth from a drawstring bag that dangled from her arm.

He turned to his sister with a big smile. "Hey, Marjorie," he said. "How'd you like to learn to embroider a handkerchief?"

* * *

"Do you see them?" Finn whispered.

Billy shook his head and ran farther up the trail above Lookout Rock. He stared past the Douglas fir trees, searching for Dannie or Buster. "Nope," he said.

It was a good thing he and Finn had dumped Marjorie with Alice Ann and Lucy. Billy chuckled to himself, thinking about how eager the girls had been to take Marjorie under their wing. Those know-it-alls couldn't resist showing off their skills with a needle. Well, that was fine with him. He and Finn still had a chance of catching up to Dannie if they hurried.

Billy looked up the trail of bare earth and packed-down pine needles. His father said that the trail had been there since Indian times. These days, people hiked up the trail from Scenic to fish along the Tye, or set traps for weasels, mink, and martens.

"Maybe we'll see Gus fishing up here too," Billy said. "He might have seen Dannie. Or at least he can tell us what Mr. Dempsey was yelling at him about."

Just then, loud splashing sounded from farther up the trail. A flash of red fur bounded out of the river.

Buster trotted along the bank with his muzzle close to the ground. His wet tail wagged happily. Dannie walked a ways behind him. She was moving very slowly. Every once in a while she turned to stare into the trees on either side of the trail.

"What's she looking for?" Finn said.

Suddenly, Buster took off into the trees, barking wildly. The shrieks of squirrels, sparrows, and nuthatches echoed through the trees.

"What is it, boy?" Dannie called.

She ran after him. Billy and Finn quickly followed. They kept close to the trees, trying not to trip over the roots that were hidden among the coltsfoot and wood sorrel plants. Billy strained to keep Dannie's bobbing black curls in sight. She finally stopped next to a steep, rocky hillside covered with weeds. The two boys ducked behind the wide branches of a fir tree.

Buster sniffed over a mound of freshly dug earth.

"Do you think that's where Mr. Renwick hid the dynamite?" Finn whispered to Billy.

Billy shrugged. Dannie was crouching over the dirt now. When she straightened up again, she held something crumpled and white in her hands.

Paper? he wondered. Whatever it was, Dannie looked at it carefully for a minute. Then she put the white object in her shirt pocket and started back toward the trail.

"Come on, Buster," Dannie called. "We're done here."

Buster loped toward a spot farther up the trail. Luckily, Dannie followed the dog instead of doubling back past him and Finn. The boys waited until she was almost out of sight before continuing behind her.

Dannie kept to the trail, which twisted alongside the river. Occasionally she stepped out of sight behind a rock or a thick group of trees.

"Where is she this time?" Finn murmured.

Dannie seemed to have disappeared. The boys could see the sparkling blue waters of Crystal Lake ahead. A trail wound in and out of sight, but Billy didn't see Dannie or Buster anywhere on it.

The two boys ran ahead to the lake, which spilled into the Tye. Water tumbled noisily over a waterfall. A log had fallen across the end of the river, just in front of the falls. One end of the log rested on a large, flat rock hemmed in by bushy fir trees.

"Let's try this way," Billy said. He stepped carefully onto the log.

He and Finn were halfway across when Dannie suddenly burst from the trees. In her hands was a long tree branch. She rushed at the boys, swinging the branch low in the air.

Thwack!

Billy yowled as the branch struck him in the shins. It knocked his feet right out from under him. The lake and trees spun around him in swirls of blue, green, and brown.

Then ice-cold water closed over Billy's head.

CHAPTER TEN

FRIEND—OR ENEMY?

B illy struggled in the freezing water. His arms and legs felt numb and clumsy. His sopping clothes and boots were like weights that dragged him down. Somehow he managed to kick toward the surface. He broke through the water, gasping for air.

"H-help!" Billy sputtered through chattering teeth.

"Grab onto the branch!" Finn called. "Hurry, before you hit the falls!"

Billy felt the pull of the current. The rocks of the falls were just in front of him. Out of the corner of his eye, he saw Finn yank Dannie's branch from her. He held the branch in front of Billy, and Billy grabbed it. He hung on while Finn pulled him to the rock where Dannie stood. A moment later, Billy lay flat on his back in a puddle of water.

A dark shadow blocked the warm rays of the sun.

Billy opened one eye and saw Dannie standing over him.

"Are you okay?" she asked.

Billy sat up. "Yeah. No thanks to you."

Danny crossed her arms and scowled. "Why are you sneaking around after my father and me?" she demanded.

"Us? What about *you?"* Billy cried. *"You're* the ones running around with dynamite and blowing up buildings."

Dannie bent closer to Billy, shaking her fist. "Take that back, or I'll throw you in again!" she said. Finn dragged her away.

"We saw you with dynamite, Dannie," Finn said. "We saw your father trying to break into the security office, too. Right before he tried to kill us with a boulder!"

Now Dannie whirled angrily to face Finn. "Papa wasn't breaking in. And he didn't try to kill anyone!" she insisted.

"That's a lie, and you know it," Billy shot back. He wrung water from his dripping shirt, then looked Dannie straight in the face. "You followed us. You saw the whole thing. Believe me, your father will be fired in a second when the railroad company finds out what he's up to."

"Fired?" Dannie said. For the first time, a glimmer of fear replaced the fury in her eyes. "They c-can't fire him!" she said. "Papa didn't do anything!"

Finn and Billy looked at each other and said nothing.

"Honest! My father went to the security office to see Mr. Jenkins about a job," Dannie rushed on. "He wasn't breaking in. When he heard you he got spooked and ran away, that's all."

"My father says the only kind of man who runs from things is the kind who's got something to hide," Finn said.

"Anyhow, your father's already got a job," Billy pointed out. "Why does he need another one?"

"It's for my brother Mike." Dannie snapped a sprig of needles from the fir tree behind her. Buster sniffed at the branches.

"We owed a lot of money when we left Chicago," Dannie went on. "My mother was sick for a long time before she..." Dannie blinked. "Before she died. It cost a lot of money, and the banks wouldn't give Papa a loan. He had to borrow it from...well, from some bad guys."

"You mean, gangsters?" Billy asked.

Dannie nodded. "Papa couldn't pay them back," she said quietly. "That's why we need to earn all we can here in Scenic."

"Jeepers!" Finn said. "Don't tell me you skipped town without paying the money back?"

Dannie looked down at the ground. "Papa will pay up as quick as he can. I know he will!" she said, lifting her chin. "But he gets scared sometimes. He's afraid the people he owes will come looking for him before he's got all the money."

So *that* was the trouble Mr. Renwick didn't want following them from Chicago, Billy thought. He felt sorry for Dannie. But he could think of plenty of questions she hadn't answered.

"But what about the dynamite?" he asked. "And the boulder he pushed down the mountain at us? He could have killed us!"

"That wasn't Papa," Dannie insisted. "Honest. He never even went up the mountain at all. He went straight home from the security office."

Her voice was clear and firm. Billy wanted to believe her. Then he remembered that Dannie had run away after the boulder nearly crushed them, too.

"What about *you?*" he said. "I know you were following us."

"So what if I was?" Dannie said. Her eyes flashed. "I was steaming mad when I saw you sneak out after my father. So I followed you. That boulder really scared me, too! I didn't know what to do. When I saw you were all right, I ran home. That's where I found Papa."

Finn frowned. "Well, if your father was in your cabin," he said slowly, "then who pushed that boulder at us?"

"That's what I've been trying to find out!" Dannie said. "So I can prove once and for all Papa didn't have a thing to do with any dynamite."

She whistled for Buster, and the dog came bounding out of the trees. "I never even saw the stuff in my life before Buster found that stick," she went on. "I wouldn't have touched it if I'd known what it was."

"Buster found it?" said Finn. "Where?"

Dannie shrugged. "Don't know. He took off into the woods on Saturday while Papa and Mike and I were unpacking. When he came back, he had it in his mouth. I didn't think anything about it 'til you two started treating me like I just robbed a bank. Then, after that big explosion..."

"You decided to find out who stole the dynamite so your family wouldn't get blamed?" Billy guessed.

Dannie nodded. "I figured Buster must have gotten the dynamite from wherever the crate was hidden. Since someone wanted to stop you two from climbing past Lookout Rock, I thought the hiding place might be someplace up here."

That made sense, Billy had to admit. "What about that place you stopped at back there?" he asked her. "Did you see the crate?"

"All I found was this." Dannie pulled a crumpled piece of paper from the pocket of her shirt. "Looks like some kind of map."

Billy shivered in his sopping clothes as he stared at the paper. Someone had drawn a bunch of lines and symbols on it. "There's Lookout Rock," he said. "And there's the trail up to Crystal Lake."

"What are all those Xs?" Finn asked. He pointed at the marks scattered across the paper. Billy figured there were at least a dozen.

"Don't know," Dannie said. "But they can't all be places where the dynamite's hidden, can they?"

"Hmm." Billy gazed out over Crystal Lake. A hawk circled high overhead. A pair of swimming ducks sent tiny waves rippling across the surface. Two black-tailed deer stepped to the water's edge and bent to drink.

Suddenly, a boom echoed in the distance. The deer's heads shot up in alarm.

"Oh, no!" Billy cried. He saw fear on Finn's face—and Dannie's, too.

"More dynamite!" Finn said. "It's happened again!"

Chapter Eleven

TOUGH TIMES IN SCENIC

That blast could have come from anywhere," Billy said. He immediately thought of his family. "What if someone was hurt?"

The thick trees blocked their view of Scenic. But smoke was rising into the air.

"We need to get back to camp right away!" Dannie said. She whistled for Buster. "Come on, boy!"

She, Billy, and Finn ran back across the log to the trail. Buster raced ahead. To Billy, it seemed like forever before the tar paper roofs and wood-sided buildings of the camp came into sight. As the three of them neared Lookout Rock, they were finally able to see where the trail of smoke was coming from.

"The tunnel entrance!" Finn said, pointing.

From all over Scenic, men hurried toward the tunnel. Billy, Finn, and Dannie raced past the school and family cabins to the road. As they got closer to the tunnel, they saw that the tunnel itself was untouched. The smoke and flames were coming from *beyond* the tunnel entrance. Billy blinked into the stinging, smoky air.

"Oh, no," he breathed.

Fifty feet from the tunnel entrance, a huge crater had been blown in the ground. Dirt, pine needles, rocks, and shrubs had blasted out of the hole. The nearby brush was on fire. Crackling flames were spreading out in a ring. Billy gasped when he saw the storage shed that stood straight in the path of the flames. Two words were painted on the door in bright red letters: DANGER! EXPLOSIVES.

"That building will blow sky high!" Finn cried.

The heat from the fire seeped through Billy's soggy clothes. But he couldn't stop shivering. He, Finn, and Dannie quickly moved off the road to make room for the truck that carried Scenic's water pump and hose. There was a mad rush of shouting as men worked to get the hose operating. Billy saw his father standing just beyond the flames. Mr. Cole had a bandanna knotted over his nose and mouth. He and a dozen other men used saws and axes to hack at the trees and bushes. Mr. Jenkins stood nearby, red-faced and sweaty. He shouted instructions to those who were just arriving.

"Clear the area around the shed!" he said. "If that building catches fire..."

"Papa!" Dannie shouted suddenly.

Mr. Renwick was running out of the storage shed with a crate of dynamite in his arms. He frowned when he saw Dannie.

"Get home, Dannie. It's too dangerous here," he told her.

Then he saw Billy and Finn, and his frown deepened to a scowl. Without another word, he ran with the crate to a truck that was parked on the road behind them. Other men followed with more crates. Dannie's father placed his crate on the truck bed.

"Get home now, Dannie," he said again. Then he turned and headed toward the tunnel entrance.

Why was he going *there?* Billy wondered.

Just then, Marjorie ran up and grabbed his hand. "Billy!" she cried. "Alice Ann and Lucy said there was a 'splosion!"

Alice Ann and Lucy were right behind her. "Was it dynamite?" Alice Ann asked.

Finn nodded.

"Hey! This is no place for kids," a voice barked. "Get on out of here!"

Billy turned to see Mr. Jenkins waving his arms at them.

"Can't you see there's dynamite here? It's dangerous!" he sputtered. He motioned Billy and the others away from the fire. "Go on home to your mothers right now. All of you!"

"Y-yes, sir," Alice Ann said. She and Lucy turned and walked quickly away, but Billy held back.

"Come *on,* Billy." Marjorie tugged on his hand.

Billy still didn't move. Men were starting to douse the flames with the hose. Mr. Jenkins rushed over to them, shouting something Billy couldn't hear.

"You know what, Finn?" he said. "Whoever blew up the garage had to have done this, too."

Finn nodded, staring at the smoking crater. "Too bad *we're* the only ones who care about finding out who it is," he said. Then he blinked in surprise. "Hey! I see something!"

He began to run straight toward the fire.

"Finn, wait!" Billy called to his friend. "Are you crazy?"

"Hey, kid! Get out of there!" someone shouted.

Finn darted around some burning bushes. He plucked something from beneath the fiery branches, then ran back to Billy.

In his hands was a blackened bundle. Dangling from it was a smoking wedge of wood. The letters SIVES were printed on it.

"It's the top of the dynamite crate!" Finn said breathlessly. "The one we saw in the school shed!"

"And look!" Billy poked at the bundle of cloth. "Red plaid," he said. "Or it used to be, anyway."

The pattern was an exact match to the scrap he had found outside the school shed. The fabric was hot to the touch, but Billy grabbed it and pulled. Two sleeves flapped out from the half-burned body of a shirt.

Finn reached down and poked a finger through a hole that was ripped out of the elbow of one sleeve. "There's a name written on the collar, too," he said.

Billy knew the men who lived in the bunkhouses labeled their clothes. That way their things didn't get mixed up when they were laundered. He looked at the name that was inked inside the collar. The letters were hard to make out.

"Frank Dempsey!" he breathed finally.

"Finn! Billy!"

Billy turned to see his father striding toward them. His mouth was still covered by his bandanna, but his eyes flashed with annoyance.

"Daddy!" Marjorie held up a white cloth. The first letters of the alphabet were embroidered on it in uneven stitches. "Look what I made with Alice Ann and Lucy!"

Their father took no notice. He yanked his bandanna

down, uncovering his mouth. "Is this how you take care of your little sister, Billy?" he said. "By bringing her here?" He nodded at the smoking crate top and shirt. "Drop those things. Now."

"But, Mr. Cole," Finn began. "These are real important! Just let us explain...."

"I've had enough of your explanations," Billy's father said impatiently. He grabbed the crate lid and shirt without looking at them. "Go on home, all of you. I don't want to have to tell you again. Billy, tell your mother I'll be back when I can."

* * *

It was long after supper before Billy's father stepped through the front door of their cabin. Marjorie was already in bed. Billy and Finn were sprawled on the rug in the front room, listening to the radio.

Usually, the two boys were hungry for every word of *Sam 'n' Henry*. From day to day, they followed the hard times and adventures of the two country bumpkins trying to get along in the big city. But tonight, Billy had a hard time concentrating on the show. When he saw his father's face, tired and covered with grime, he forgot about Sam and Henry altogether.

"These sure are tough times, Ruth," said Mr. Cole. He walked with heavy steps to the kitchen, where Billy's mother was thumbing through the Sears, Roebuck catalog. "Two explosions in two days. And we still don't know who's behind this trouble."

Billy's mother said something in a low voice while she took a plate from the oven.

"If someone wanted to destroy the tunnel, he'd have set off that dynamite *inside* the mountain," Mr. Cole said.

He washed his hands and face at the kitchen sink, then sat at the table. "Whoever planted that dynamite put it near the storage shed, but not close enough to fire up the explosives," he went on. "And the explosion in the garage…It was close to the bunkhouses, but luckily it didn't damage them."

"Then no one was hurt?" Billy's mother asked anxiously.

Mr. Cole shook his head. "Seems to me this fellow's just trying to scare us all," he said. He stabbed at some chicken with his fork. "For the life of me, I can't guess why."

"Why don't you ask Frank Dempsey, Mr. Cole?" Finn spoke up from the rug.

Billy's father turned to frown at the two boys.

"It was Frank's shirt we found, Dad," Billy added quickly. "With part of the dynamite crate. You took them from us up at the fire, remember? Mr. Dempsey must be the one who set off the dynamite!"

Mr. Cole rubbed his temples. "When are you boys going to learn to leave this business alone?" he said tiredly.

"Are we going to 'splode?" a small, sleepy voice spoke up from the doorway.

Billy turned to see Marjorie standing there in her nightgown. Her hair was tousled. She rubbed her eyes, yawning. Behind her were the steep stairs that led up to the attic loft where she and Billy slept.

"No, sweetie pie. Of course not," Mrs. Cole said quickly. She took Marjorie onto her lap and shot a warning glance at the boys and Billy's father.

"Good." Marjorie snuggled into her mother's arms. "Because I want Billy to leave me with Alice Ann and Lucy again so they can teach me more 'broidery."

"What? William Edmund Cole!" Billy's mother frowned at him over the top of Marjorie's head. "Did you actually leave your little sister with—?"

"Marjorie must be so tired she doesn't know what she's saying," Billy cut in. He grabbed his sister's hand and pulled her toward the stairs. "Come on," he said.

"Finn and I will tell you a story about Sam and Henry 'til you fall back asleep."

Finn followed him and Marjorie up to the loft. Billy ducked to keep from hitting the roof beams that slanted to a point overhead. Moonlight shone in through the window, lighting up Marjorie's bed. His own bed was at the opposite end of the loft, beneath the other window.

As Marjorie climbed beneath her covers, Billy half-expected their mother to call him back for a lecture. Then he heard his father say something more about the dynamite, and his mother's softer voice answering.

"Looks like we're off the hook," Billy whispered. "No thanks to you, Marjorie."

"What did *I* do?" she asked sleepily. She pulled her blanket up under her chin. "Anyhow, I do so know what I'm talking about, Billy. You did leave me with Alice Ann and Lucy!"

"*Shhh!*" Billy glanced toward the stairs. Luckily, his parents were still talking.

"Stop being such a little blabbermouth," he told her. "Now hush up, so we can tell you that story."

Finn winked at Billy. "Should we tell her the one where Sam and Henry meet a little girl who goes to jail for blabbing secrets?" he said.

Marjorie's lip began to tremble. "I don't like that story," she said in a small voice.

Billy softened. "Well, I *guess* we can change it," he said, tweaking her nose. "You just watch what you say to Mother and Dad from now on, all right?"

He and Finn had no trouble thinking of funny Sam and Henry stories. Marjorie smiled when they told her about Sam's funny letters to his sweetheart back in Alabama. But Billy's mind kept wandering.

He couldn't stop thinking about Frank Dempsey's shirt and the piece of the dynamite crate. Weren't they proof enough that Frank had taken the dynamite? Why couldn't his father see that?

Guess it's up to Finn and me to prove it, he told himself. Then another thought popped into his head.

What about Dannie? Billy wondered. Could they count on her to help?

Chapter Twelve

THE OLD TRAIN ROBBERY

Miss Wrigley's classroom was buzzing with excitement on Monday morning.

"Guess what?" Billy heard Janet tell Alice Ann. "Lucy's mother kept her out of school today. She's afraid someone will set off more dynamite."

"Children, *please!*" Miss Wrigley said. She clapped her hands. "We can't let any trouble at the camp interrupt our studies."

Alice Ann was the first to take her seat. Miss Wrigley had to ask everyone else three times. Finally, the other girls and boys went to their desks. Only Dannie remained standing.

"Class, I'd like you to welcome a new student to school today," Miss Wrigley said, smiling warmly. "Daniella Renwick and her family have just moved here from Chicago. I'm sure you'll all make Daniella feel at home here in Scenic."

Dannie shifted uncomfortably. "Everyone calls me Dannie," she said quietly.

There were a few murmurs of "hello" from the other kids. But Billy had the feeling everyone was too busy thinking about the dynamite to pay much attention to Dannie. Finally Miss Wrigley led her to Alice Ann's desk in the front row.

"Alice Ann, would you please show Daniella where we are in our speller?" Miss Wrigley asked.

Alice Ann slid over to make room for Dannie. "I'll help you get started with today's lesson. I *am* the best student in our class, after all," she said, giving Dannie a big smile. "We'll be great friends, I'm sure, Daniella."

"Dannie," Dannie snapped.

Billy could see that Dannie wasn't nearly as impressed with Alice Ann as Lucy and Janet were. She just rolled her eyes while Alice Ann showed her the day's lessons. As soon as the other girls began to study, Dannie turned around. She glanced past Lucy and Janet—straight at Billy.

"We need to find out more about that Frank Dempsey," she whispered.

"Daniella." Alice Ann tapped Dannie on the shoulder. "I mean, *Dannie,* we're not allowed to talk," she said.

Dannie paid no attention to Alice Ann. "There's got to be a way to prove that Frank is the one who took the dynamite," she said to Billy.

Wes glanced up from his book, but Billy ignored him. "Right," he whispered back.

The truth was, he and Finn had already come up with a plan. But Billy wasn't sure he was ready to share it with Dannie. Not until he knew for sure her father wasn't mixed up with the missing dynamite.

"We could follow him," Dannie said.

"That's what Billy wants to do!" Finn said, before Billy could stop him. Finn leaned forward from the desk behind Billy's. "We figured we could track Mr. Dempsey down at lunch and—"

Alice Ann cleared her throat loudly.

"Daniella, Finn, and Billy!" Miss Wrigley called out. She stepped away from the board, where she had been writing out spelling words for the first and second graders. "Are you done studying? I'll quiz you now on your lesson."

None of them could spell a single word. Billy squirmed under their teacher's stern gaze. He squirmed even more when she told him, Finn, and

Dannie they would have to stay in during lunch to review their lesson.

"Today?" Billy said. But he knew exactly what Miss Wrigley's answer would be.

"Today," she said. "And if you don't learn it fully, you'll stay after school as well."

"Yes, ma'am." Billy thumped against his chair and looked back at Finn.

So much for their big plan to follow Frank Dempsey.

At lunch, Miss Wrigley called Dannie up to her desk. The other children were eating or playing outside. Billy looked out the window and saw Alice Ann, Lucy, and Janet sitting on the schoolhouse fence. Buster sat under a tree nearby. The dog was watching the schoolhouse with expectant eyes.

"Daniella," Billy heard Miss Wrigley say in a low voice, "I had hoped you might follow a better example. I'm sure Alice Ann would...."

Billy tuned out the rest of their conversation. He and Finn were halfway through their sandwiches when Dannie returned to her desk.

"I don't guess we can all be as perfect as that Alice Ann Lockhart," she grumbled. "Miss Wrigley says I should get to know some nice girls here at Scenic, since I haven't got a mother or a sister."

A sad look came into Dannie's eyes. But she shook it away.

"Anyhow, she lent me this." Dannie plunked a slender book down on Billy's desk. "So I can learn more about the area around Scenic. Miss Wrigley's mother wrote it."

Billy peered at the title on the cover: *A Cascades History. By Irene Felsom Wrigley.*

He flipped open the cover and read the first paragraph:

Oh! The majestic heights of our glorious Cascades! Who among us has not marveled at the sight? Yet those impressive peaks house so much more than Nature's bounty. They house a history of the pioneer spirit—the same spirit that forged our great country. It is the stories of those wonderful pioneers, passed on by generations of Wrigleys, that I relate in these pages.

"I guess being a know-it-all runs in the family," Billy said, grinning. He handed the book back to Dannie and turned back to his speller.

Dannie flipped through the pages. "Hey! There was a train robbery here in 1893!" she said. She walked back to her desk, still reading. "It says that the outlaws got away with a fortune in gold coins."

"Really?" Finn leaned forward. "Did they catch the men who did it?"

Dannie checked the book again. "Everyone in the gang went to jail," she said. "Except for the ringleader, a scoundrel named Fingers McGee. He got away with most of the gold."

"That's him?" Billy pointed to a picture that filled a whole page of the book. It showed an old poster. WANTED was spelled out at the top in old-fashioned letters. FRANK "FINGERS" McGEE was printed under it.

The face that stared out from the poster was surly and dark. A hat was pulled low over the man's forehead. Strands of greasy-looking dark hair covered his ears and cheeks. There was a sharp glimmer in the man's eyes that made Billy shiver.

"'Age 27. Black hair, blue eyes, scar two inches long behind the left ear...'" he read. "Wonder how he got that?"

"Miss Wrigley?" Finn called out. "About that old train robbery... No one ever found Fingers McGee *or* the gold?" he asked.

Miss Wrigley glanced up from her desk. "Well, it's nice to see you children are taking *some* interest in learning," she said. "Even if it isn't your assigned topic." She raised an eyebrow at Finn, but Billy saw their teacher smile at the sight of them reading her mother's book.

"And no, Fingers McGee was never caught," Miss Wrigley went on. "Some of the gold was recovered from his band of outlaws, but he got away with most of it. Local legend has it that he buried his loot somewhere near Scenic. People have dug up half the mountainside searching for it over the years. But no one has ever found any gold."

"Hey!" Dannie sat straight up. "What about that dug-up spot Buster found yesterday?" she whispered to Billy and Finn.

"You think someone was looking for Fingers McGee's gold?" Billy asked.

"Sure," Finn said excitedly. "Why else would there be a map? Those *X*s we saw were probably places where the person already looked."

"Maybe," Billy said slowly. Then a picture popped into his head. "Finn! Remember when we saw Mr. Dempsey, right after the first explosion? He was all covered in dirt. And he was carrying a shovel."

Finn nodded. "You bet. He sure did look like he'd been digging."

"Children," Miss Wrigley cut in. "I'm afraid I'll have to ask you to put away that history book until later.

Unless you're ready to be tested on your spelling words?"

Dannie, Finn, and Billy looked at one another.

"Um, no, ma'am," Dannie said. With a sigh, she closed A Cascades History and turned back to her speller.

Billy stumbled through his lessons for the rest of the day. A dozen new questions spun inside his head. He was dying to talk them over with Finn. As soon as Mr. Farnam rang the end-of-school bell, Billy dragged his friend away from the other kids.

"Let's go to the cookhouse," he said. "We need a snack while we figure out what to do."

The cookhouse was one of the boys' regular stops after school. Tommy and Gil, the bakers who worked under Chef Whitman, almost always set aside broken or cracked cookies for them.

"Wait up!" Dannie called. She ran up behind them with her lunch pail as Buster jumped at her side.

Billy hesitated. He was starting to like Dannie. But he still wasn't sure about her father. "What do you think, Finn?" he said to his friend in a low voice.

Dannie heard him. She stopped in her tracks, frowning. "Don't tell me you still think Papa's mixed up with those explosions?" she said. "He's not! Didn't you hear anything I told you yesterday, Billy Cole?"

Billy just stood there.

Dannie leaned down to scratch Buster behind the ears. "I guess we're about as unlucky as Sam and Henry, eh, boy?" she said.

"What?" Billy blinked, surprised. "You listen to *Sam 'n' Henry?*"

"What do you care?" Dannie said. "At least folks in the big city gave those guys a chance. That's more than anyone here is doing for Papa and Mike and me. Well, if you don't want my help, that's just fine with me! Come on, Buster."

She turned and began to storm off.

"Wait!" Finn called. He looked at Billy. "She gave us the map, Billy," he said. "Who knows? Maybe she's right about someone looking for Fingers McGee's gold."

Billy had to admit it was possible. He looked Dannie straight in the eye. Solemnly, he spit into his palm and held it out to her. "Do you swear you're telling the truth?" he asked.

Dannie nodded. "I swear," she said. Then she spit into her own palm and shook Billy's hand.

"Okay then," Finn said, grinning. "Let's get some cookies!"

* * *

Ten minutes later, the three of them sat on the platform outside the cookhouse with a handful of cookies.

"We've got two things to think about," Billy said. "First off, there's a pretty good chance Frank Dempsey has that missing crate of dynamite. And now it looks like he's digging for the gold from that old train robbery, too!"

Dannie held half a cookie out to Buster. Crumbs fell from the dog's mouth as he gulped it down. "If you saw Frank with a shovel," she said, "maybe he's the one who was digging where I found this."

She reached to the pile of books and lunch pails behind them on the platform. The crumpled map stuck out from between the pages of her history book.

"Well, here's what I can't figure out," Billy said. He leaned back against the pine siding of the cookhouse. "What do the missing dynamite and the gold have to do with each another?"

"I see what you mean," Finn said slowly. "If Frank is digging for gold up on the mountain, why would he set off dynamite down here in the camp?"

The door to the cookhouse swung open. Billy did a double-take as Frank Dempsey himself stepped onto the platform.

"You kids again?" he said, scowling. "Don't you know when to scram?"

Frank didn't wait for an answer. He stalked off toward the bunkhouses.

"Should we go after him?" Dannie whispered.

Billy grabbed his lunch pail and books and jumped to his feet. "You bet!" he said.

Frank was just disappearing behind the first row of bunkhouses. As Billy, Finn, and Danny followed, they saw Gus Pratt leaving the bunkhouses. He walked toward them.

"Hey there," Gus said. "You boys thinking of fishing this afternoon?"

"Um..." Finn shot an anxious glance toward the bunkhouses.

"Not really, Mr. Pratt," Billy spoke up. "We're, um...we're kind of busy right now."

"That so?" Gus turned to follow Billy's gaze. "Well, I might head up the river myself after I grab some chow," he said. He raked his fingers through his white hair.

"Sure, Mr. Pratt," Billy said. He was eager to get going. Finn and Dannie were already turning down the row of bunkhouses ahead of him. "See you later."

Billy began to follow his friends—then stopped. He stared at the left side of Gus's head.

There, just behind the old man's left ear, was a scar. About two inches long!

CHAPTER THIRTEEN

TRAILING SUSPECTS

Billy? Are you all right?" Gus asked.

The old man was staring at Billy. Billy shook himself and tore his eyes away from Gus's scar. "Um, sure, Mr. Pratt," he said. "I, uh, I gotta go!"

His heart pounded as he raced down the walkway. When he reached the first row of bunkhouses, he glanced back. Gus was just disappearing inside the cookhouse. Billy turned the corner and saw Finn and Dannie a few yards ahead of him. Frank Dempsey was even farther down the walkway.

"Finn! Dannie!" Billy called in a hoarse whisper. He caught up to his friends and told them about Gus's scar.

"What!" Finn and Dannie both exclaimed.

"Think about it," said Billy. "Mr. Pratt's got blue eyes, just like Fingers McGee."

"Lots of folks have blue eyes," Dannie pointed out.

"Sure, but what about the scar?" Billy said. "The one Mr. Pratt has fits the description on the wanted poster perfectly!"

Finn let out a low whistle. "Do you *really* think he's Fingers McGee? I mean, Mr. Pratt's always been so nice to us. He's our friend."

"I'm just saying it's possible, that's all." Billy said. "Mr. Pratt's hair is white now, but it might have been black before. After all, the train was robbed way back in 1893. Mr. Pratt would have been a lot younger then."

"About the same age as Fingers McGee," Finn said slowly. "But if Mr. Pratt is Fingers McGee, why would he wait so long to dig up that gold he hid? He would have taken it a long time ago!"

"Besides, one little scar isn't proof," Dannie said. "Papa has lots of scars. And we've got Mr. Dempsey to keep our eye on, too, you know. He's acting pretty funny."

"It was Frank's name on that shirt, not Mr. Pratt's," Finn added.

Billy stared down the walkway ahead of them. Twenty bunkhouses stretched along each side. Frank was just walking through the doorway of the last bunkhouse on the left.

"You're right," Billy said with a sigh. "Let's go!"

They ran down the walkway to the last bunkhouse. Just as they reached it, the door swung open.

"What do you pesky kids want now?" Frank demanded.

He took a step toward them. Buster bent low over his front paws and growled, but Frank didn't flinch. His face was filled with menace. "Why, I ought to..."

Frank suddenly stopped talking. "Hey!" he said. His hand shot toward the books Dannie held under her arm. He snatched the map from between the pages of her history book. "What are you doing with this?"

"Is that your map, Mr. Dempsey?" Finn asked.

"Darned right." Frank shoved the map into the pocket of his trousers. "I ought to tell your fathers you pint-sized troublemakers are taking things that don't belong to you."

"Go ahead!" Dannie said. Her cheeks burned as she faced Frank. "And while you're at it, you can explain why *your* shirt was found where the dynamite was set off yesterday!"

"*My* shirt?" Frank let out a snort. "Ha! That's a good one."

He turned on his heel and strode inside the bunkhouse. A moment later, he came back to the doorway with a charred bundle of red-plaid fabric. Billy recognized the shirt Finn had found at the tunnel. A smoky odor tickled his nose as Frank shook out the shirt and held it up. It didn't begin to cover Frank's chest.

"That shirt wouldn't fit you in a million years," said Finn, frowning. "It's too small!"

"That's exactly what I told your fathers when they called me in this morning for an explanation," Frank said.

"Our fathers?" Billy said. He was glad to know his dad and Mr. Mackenzie were trying to find out who had stolen the dynamite and set off the blasts. But what if they didn't find the person fast enough?

"I don't get it," Billy said. "Your name's on that shirt, Mr. Dempsey. Even if it is too small."

"It's obviously someone's way of putting the blame on me for all the no-good business around here," Frank said.

"Wait a minute. Are you saying someone else wrote your name in the shirt and put it with the piece of crate?" Dannie asked.

"That's right," Frank said, nodding. "All that low-down skunk had to do was leave it where folks would find it. Next thing you know, everyone thinks I set off the dynamite."

Billy shifted from one boot to the other. "Um, we might know who did it, Mr. Dempsey," he said.

"You mean Mr. Pratt, right, Billy?" Finn blurted out. Then he covered his mouth with his hand. "Oops."

"Gus Pratt? That's a laugh," Frank scoffed. "That geezer doesn't have the brains to set me up. He can barely find his way back here to his bunk after the night shift."

Dannie looked past Frank, into the bunkhouse. "His bunk is in *here?*" she asked. "Can we see it?"

Frank shrugged. "Suit yourselves," he said, stepping back so they could enter.

"You stay here, Buster," Dannie said. Then she followed Billy and Finn inside.

Billy had never seen so many beds in one place. There were twelve in all, jammed against the walls with a narrow walking space between them. Clothing hung from hooks. Books and other personal items were piled on crates that served as tables. Most of the bunks were empty, but Billy saw two men lying on their beds with newspapers. Two more men were playing checkers on another bunk.

"Kids got no place in here," one of them muttered. Frank glared at him, and the man didn't say anything more.

Frank led Dannie, Finn, and Billy to the back of the room. "That's Pratt's bunk. Turn it upside down, for all I care," he said. Then he went over to his own bed and flopped down on it.

Billy, Finn, and Dannie wasted no time. Billy looked through the pants and workshirts that hung above Gus's bed. Dannie felt under the mattress while Finn combed through the things that were stowed below it.

"Hey! What's this?" Finn said.

He sat back on his heels with Gus's leather tackle bag. The flap was open. Billy watched closely as his friend slipped his fingers into a narrow slit at the base of the flap. Finn pulled out a piece of paper marked with faded, blotched ink.

"*Another* map?" Dannie said. "It sure does look old."

Billy leaned over for a closer look. The paper had turned brown with age. It was so brittle that the corners had worn off. The paper crinkled as Finn unfolded it. Billy tried to make sense of the faded and blotched markings.

The first thing he saw was the zigzag line of the switchbacks above Scenic. As he peered more closely, he recognized the old Indian trail, and Crystal Lake. There were other markings, too. But what really caught his eye were three crudely drawn sacks of coins. A name was scrawled on the map, too. Billy gasped when he read it.

"Fingers McGee!" he whispered.

"Jeepers!" Finn said. "It's the map Fingers McGee made to mark where he hid the gold!"

Dannie sat down on Gus's bunk and let out a long breath. "You were right, Billy. If Gus has the map *and* the scar, he *must* be Fingers McGee!"

CHAPTER FOURTEEN

BEAR ROCK

Billy felt as if his head would burst. Gus Pratt wasn't just a harmless old man who fished and went to the picture show with them. He was an outlaw!

"What should we do?" Billy asked Dannie and Finn.

"Let's take this map to the fort," Finn said. "We can look at it some more and figure something out."

Billy glanced over his shoulder at Frank and the other men. The two men playing checkers were arguing good-naturedly. The others had gathered around them. They didn't seem to be paying any attention at all to the three children. Billy wanted to keep it that way.

"The quicker we get out of here, the better," he whispered.

Finn stuffed the old map in his shirt pocket. Dannie put Gus's leather tackle bag back under his bunk. As the three of them moved toward the door, Frank glanced up from the checker game.

"So did you smartie kids find anything?" he asked. "Is crazy old Gus Pratt the scoundrel who's been trying to blow Scenic sky-high?"

Billy could tell Frank didn't think Gus was smart enough or dangerous enough to be the culprit. Billy decided to play along. He didn't want to spill the beans about what they'd learned. Not until they knew for sure that Frank had nothing to do with the dynamite.

"Ha, ha. That's a good one, Mr. Dempsey," Billy said, trying to smile. "Sorry we bothered you."

He, Finn, and Dannie hurried outside and jumped off the walkway to the ground below. They took the road around the edge of camp, then followed the river to the schoolhouse. Buster seemed to sense their nervousness. He turned his head at every rustle or chirp from the trees. Billy almost expected Gus to jump out and pounce on them. Even after they reached the fort, his heart thumped wildly in his chest.

"We'd better be quick," he said. "We don't know how long it'll be before Mr. Pratt realizes we've got his map."

Very carefully, Finn spread the map out on the rocky floor of the fort.

The drawing of the bags of coins was a ways from the line that marked the old Indian trail. Billy peered at the faded pictures and writing that surrounded the bags.

"The gold must be inside a cave," he said slowly. "Looks like it's set into the mountain under some big rock."

Dannie pointed at the words printed beneath the boulder. "Bear Rock."

Finn's head shot up. "Hey! I know where that is!" he said. "Mr. Farnam showed it to me once when I went with him to check his traps. It's in an old avalanche basin!"

"A what?" Dannie asked.

"An avalanche basin is what's left after a heavy snow slide," Billy explained. "A big mess of rocks and dirt that gets piled up in the path where the snow comes through."

"Oh. Then did you see any cave, Finn?" Dannie asked.

Finn shook his head. "Maybe the avalanche covered it up," he said.

Billy thought for a minute. "Hey!" he said. "If the cave *did* get covered up, Mr. Pratt would need something pretty powerful to blast through all that rock to get his gold."

"Like dynamite!" Dannie said. "Maybe *that's* why he stole that crate!"

The three of them looked at each other. "We've got to get to Bear Rock," Finn said. "Fast!"

Just then, Billy saw a small figure running along the river toward Lookout Rock.

"Billy!" the little person called out. "Mother says—"

Marjorie! Billy thought. *Oh, no!*

"Run home quick!" Billy shouted back, without giving his sister time to finish. "Tell Mother and Dad we've gone up to Bear Rock. To find Fingers McGee's gold!"

Marjorie stopped. "You're looking for gold?" she said, scrunching up her nose. "Can I play?"

"It's not a game," Billy told her firmly. "Just go! Get help!"

"You go with her, Buster!" Dannie clapped to get her dog's attention. She pointed toward Marjorie. "Go, boy! Don't worry, Marjorie. Buster'll help your mother and dad find us."

Billy, Danny, and Finn waited long enough to see Marjorie and Buster turn back toward the family cabins. Then they took off up the trail at a run.

The late afternoon sun was dropping. Long, slanting shadows fell across the forest floor. The three children moved so fast that their footsteps sent squirrels, hares, and deer running away through the trees. Just before they reached Crystal Lake, Finn turned off the path.

"This way," he said.

They moved deeper among the firs, larch, and mountain hemlock. Billy wasn't sure how far they'd gone when Finn finally stopped next to a break in the trees.

"I think this is the place," he said. He took a few steps forward, looking around uncertainly. Billy and Dannie followed.

Ahead they saw a steep hill of dirt, rocks, and rotting tree trunks. They looked as if they had been dragged down the mountainside. It was an avalanche basin, all right, thought Billy.

Rising high out of the dirt and rocks was a huge outcrop of rock. It looked like any big old rock at first. But as Billy stared at it, an image began to take shape. He could easily imagine a bear rearing up to protect her cubs.

"Bear Rock!" he said.

"Right!" Dannie ran over to the pile of dirt and stones next to the base of the rock. "The cave where Fingers McGee hid his gold must be buried under here!"

"Right again!" a deep voice spoke up from behind them.

Billy, Finn, and Dannie whirled around.

"Mr. Pratt!" Finn exclaimed.

Gus Pratt stood at the edge of the trees. In his arms was a wooden crate that was missing its lid. Billy knew what was inside even before he saw the powdery sticks.

"If anyone moves," said Gus, "I'll blow us all sky-high."

Chapter Fifteen
An Outlaw's Story

B illy hardly dared to breathe. He flinched as Gus set the crate of dynamite on the ground. The old man grabbed a rope that rested on top of the powdery sticks.

"Sorry, kids," he said, as he dragged Billy and Finn over to Dannie. "I need to make sure you don't pull any surprises."

Gus made the three of them sit at the base of Bear Rock. Dannie scowled as he pulled her hands behind her back. "We know you're Fingers McGee," she spat out.

"Well, well, is that so?" Gus said. "Aren't you kids clever? Luckily, I'll be far from Scenic before anyone *else* finds out."

He knotted the end of the rope around Dannie's wrists and pulled it tight. Then he worked the rope around the boys' ankles. Finally he got the dynamite crate. He set it down next to Bear Rock.

Finn shuddered. "W-what are you going to do, Mr. Pratt?" he asked.

Gus didn't answer. He just began digging holes in the rocky hillside next to the boulder. Each time he finished a hole, he placed a stick of dynamite in it.

"You're going to blow us up?" Dannie cried. "You can't do that!"

Gus reached for another dynamite stick. "You don't expect me to let a couple of kids stop me from getting at my gold, do you?" he said. "It's mine, you see. All mine! I earned that gold fair and square."

"You robbed a train. That's *stealing*," Finn pointed out.

"Bah!" scoffed Gus.

Billy felt a mixture of anger and fear as Gus planted five, six, then seven dynamite sticks. *Help is on the way,* he reminded himself. But how long would it take his parents to get there? Billy had to find a way to stall Gus.

"Tell me something, Mr. Pratt," he said. He couldn't bring himself to call the outlaw by his real name. "How come you left the gold here in the first place? Why didn't you just take it all with you after you robbed that train?"

Gus let out a sharp laugh. "Have you ever picked up a bag of gold?" he asked.

"No," Billy said. He shifted uncomfortably against the rock. He felt a stab of pain as his hands scraped against a sharp edge. Then an idea came to him.

If I can just cut into this rope... he thought.

He began to rub the rope against the sharp rock. Gus was so busy with the dynamite that he didn't even glance in Billy's direction.

"Gold is heavy, kid," Gus said. "I never would have gotten away if I'd tried to take it all. Look what happened to the boys in my gang. They got greedy, tried to take their full share of the gold with them. That's why they got caught."

"So you hid yours in the cave behind all this." Finn nodded to the dirt and rocks piled up next to Bear Rock.

"Oh, I took some of the coins," Gus said. "Went clear down to Nevada with them and changed my name. No one ever found out. I never took to fancy living, so that gold lasted a good long time."

Billy kept rubbing his ropes against the rock. He saw Dannie's gaze flicker to his wrists. She nodded at him to show she understood. Then she turned to Gus and said, "Well, the money had to run out sooner or later. That's why you came back to Scenic, to get the rest of it. Only finding it wasn't as easy as you thought, huh?"

"That's the truth, missie." Gus sighed. "How was I to know to whole mountain would be crawling with railroad folks now? But once I signed on as a worker at the camp, no one looked twice at me."

Gus shook his head. "Only trouble was, a mountain sure can change in thirty years. No matter how many times I hiked up from camp, I couldn't find that cave. Then I had to wait out the winter snows *and* make sure no one saw me."

"But Finn and I saw you," Billy said. "And Mr. Dempsey, when he hiked up the mountain to look for the gold himself."

Gus frowned. He reached into the crate and pulled out a long, wiry fuse. "That fool got in my way one too many times," he said. "Always coming up here with his shovel. But I took care of *him.*"

"So *you* set Frank up to take the blame for the missing dynamite!" Billy burst out. "You're the one who signed Mr. Dempsey's name. You wrote his name in your shirt after Finn and I found a scrap of it near the school shed. Then you put the shirt in the dynamite lid so someone would find it after you set off the second blast."

"That was just plain mean, Mr. Pratt," Dannie said. "People could have been hurt in those explosions. Or even killed!"

Gus threaded the fuse from one stick of dynamite to another. He didn't seem at all sorry about what he'd done. "I finally found Bear Rock on Friday," he went on calmly. "If you boys hadn't seen that dynamite, I could have blasted through to the cave that very night. I'd have gotten out with my gold before anyone at the camp was wise to me."

Billy kept scraping the rope against the rock behind his back. He felt some frayed ends, where the rock had cut into the binds. Billy yanked against them. But the ropes held firm.

"Sure, I managed to get the crate away without you seeing," Gus went on. "But I knew folks would be looking for it soon. I had to do something to keep 'em from searching up on the mountain."

"So you set off the dynamite right *in* Scenic," Billy said.

Gus nodded. "I made the fuse plenty long," he said. "That gave me time to get clear of the garage, so I wouldn't be anywhere near it when the dynamite went off. Mighty clever, huh?"

Billy could hardly believe it. Gus sounded almost proud. "Well, *I* know where you were that night," he said. "You tried to kill Finn and me with that boulder above Lookout Rock!"

"Got you two off my backs for a minute or two," Gus said. "But it wasn't enough. Seems like one thing or another kept me away. If it wasn't Dempsey digging all over the place, it was you kids nosing around for the dynamite. Well, I'll tell you one thing. I'm done waiting now."

Gus stepped back from the rock. He held the long, tangled fuse in his hands, unraveling it as he went. About fifteen feet from Bear Rock, he took a pocket-knife and a match from the pocket of his denim pants. He cut the fuse, then struck a match against the metal of his belt buckle to light it.

Fear shot through Billy like lightning. *Break, ropes!* he thought frantically. He rubbed the ropes even harder against the sharp rock behind him. His wrists were raw by now, but he kept at it. Again, he yanked against the ropes. But they still wouldn't give.

"Mr. Pratt, stop!" Dannie cried.

Gus didn't turn or answer. He held the match to the fuse, and sparks shot out from the end of it. The flame sputtered quickly toward the sticks of dynamite that jutted from the rocky earth right next to Billy, Finn, and Dannie.

"Say good-bye to Scenic, kiddies," said Gus.

Then he disappeared into the trees.

Chapter Sixteen

RACE AGAINST TIME

Nooooo!" Billy shouted.

The fuse had already burned down a few feet. In another minute the dynamite would blow!

Billy yanked at the rope one more time. It cut painfully into his raw wrists. Then...

Pop!

"I'm loose!" he cried to Finn and Dannie.

Billy shook his hands free and started tugging frantically at the rope around his ankles.

"Hurry!" Finn's voice was almost a squeak.

Billy saw the sputtering flame, just a few feet from the dynamite now. Finn and Dannie were twisting and pulling against their ropes, too. If only they had more time!

"There!" Billy kicked free of the rope.

He jumped to Finn, then Dannie, unwinding the rope

from their ankles. Their hands were still tied behind their backs. Billy took one last glance at the fuse—and gasped. It had burned almost all the way down.

"We've got to get out of here...*now!*"

He yanked on the rope, pulling Finn and Dannie to their feet. Billy pushed them toward the trees. Finn and Dannie ran clumsily, with the long rope dangling from their tied wrists.

"Faster!" Billy yelled.

BOOM! BOOM! BOOM!

The blasts sent Billy flying through the air. He hit the ground with a thud, then curled into a ball. Dirt and rocks hit him with such force that Billy almost passed out.

When it was over, a powerful silence surrounded him.

"F-Finn? Dannie?" Billy called. His voice was muffled by the heavy layer of dirt and rocks that covered him. Slowly, he shook it off and pushed himself to sit up. His whole body hurt.

"*Ooooh.*" A moan escaped from a pile of dirt a few feet away. Then the pile moved. Dirt and pebbles rolled off Dannie as she sat up. Finn appeared out of the dirt right next to her. There was a cut on his cheek. He and Dannie both looked as dazed as Billy felt.

Then Finn sucked in his breath. His eyes were fixed on something behind Billy. "Mr. Pratt!" he whispered.

Billy whirled around. A cloud of smoke was clearing from in front of Bear Rock. A crater had blown out of the ground next to the rock. It was littered with smoking rocks, dirt, and trees. Billy imagined that the battlefields in Europe during the Great War might have looked just like it.

He scowled when he saw Gus Pratt scramble across the smoking ground. The outlaw was heading straight for a ragged hole that had blasted out of the hillside right next to Bear Rock.

"The cave!" Billy said.

Clumps of dirt and pebbles dropped from the opening as Gus ran through and disappeared from sight.

"He's getting the gold!" Dannie whispered. She jumped up, but the rope binding her to Finn caused her to stumble back again. "Quick, untie us," she told Billy. "We've got to stop him!"

Billy had the rope off his friends in no time. He hung onto it as he, Finn, and Dannie ran to the hole next to Bear Rock. The sting of dynamite hung on the air. Billy stifled a sneeze as he peered cautiously through the opening.

The first thing he saw was a yellow glow farther

inside the cave. Gus had brought a flashlight with him. The beam lit up scuttling insects and rock walls dripping with moisture. The roof of the cave was just above Gus's head. The closed-in feel of the place made Billy gulp. But when Finn stepped into the cave, Billy didn't hesitate. He and Dannie were right behind him.

All of a sudden, Gus stopped. He shined his light on a mound on the cave floor. To Billy, it looked like nothing more than a dusty rock. Then Gus bent over the mound, and Billy heard the tinkle of cascading coins.

"The gold!" Dannie said. Then she clapped a hand to her mouth. "Oops," she whispered.

Gus whirled around.

"You again!" he said. His eyes were wide with disbelief.

Dropping his flashlight, Gus charged at them.

Billy flinched. But he knew what to do. His fingers tightened around the rope.

"Finn, take this!" Billy slapped one end of the rope into Finn's palm. Then he stepped back so the rope stretched between them at knee level. "Remember how Dannie got me into Crystal Lake with that branch?" he said.

Dannie jumped in front of the rope. "Right here,

Mr. Gold Robber," she taunted. She made a face at him and stuck out her tongue. "Come and get us!"

Gus scowled and came rushing at her. Just before he reached her, Dannie jumped over the rope and ducked to the side of the cave. Gus hit the rope at a full run.

"Ooomph!" He flipped over the rope and slammed down to the rocky cave floor. Then he lay motionless on the ground.

"He's out cold!" Finn said.

"Good," Billy said. He turned toward the entrance of the cave. "Did you hear something?"

The sounds of barking echoed faintly.

"Buster!" Dannie cried.

Billy heard voices, too, calling their names. He, Finn, and Dannie ran to the cave entrance to see Buster loping toward them. Mr. and Mrs. Cole hurried through the trees behind the dog. Billy had never been happier to see his parents in his life.

"We're all right!" he called, waving. "Everything's just fine."

* * *

Billy never would have expected all the fuss that followed. Newspaper men came from as far as Skykomish,

Wenatchee, Seattle, and even Chicago to take their picture. Telegrams arrived from the railroad company. The president himself thanked Billy, Finn, and Dannie for recovering the gold that had been stolen from them so many years ago. A whole squad of police from Skykomish stood guard over the coins for two days in Cal Jenkins's office. Then the railroad company shipped the treasure off to Chicago on the Northern Express.

"Well, I'll be!" Billy's mother said, when Mr. Cole showed her the Wenatchee *Daily World.*

The headline read: LOCAL HEROES FIND LONG-LOST GOLD! Cascades Outlaw Behind Bars at Last. Underneath was a photograph of Billy, Finn, and Dannie standing next to five sacks of gold coins. Each of them held up a single glistening coin that the railroad company had given them as a reward.

Billy thought he would burst with pride. When he, Finn, and Dannie walked into the schoolhouse Thursday morning, the other children crowded around them.

"What are you going to do with your gold?" Wes asked eagerly.

"Gee, I don't know," Billy said. Finn just shrugged, but Dannie said, "I gave mine to Papa."

"What? Why didn't you keep it?" Janet asked.

Dannie wouldn't say, but Billy knew why. That gold coin sure would help the Renwicks to pay off their debt in Chicago.

"Gold, gold, gold. Is that all anyone can talk about?" Alice Ann said. She walked away from the excited faces that clustered around Billy, Finn, and Dannie. "Haven't we made enough of a fuss over this?" She sat down at her desk and crossed her arms.

"Why Alice Ann," Miss Wrigley said, turning to her in surprise. "We have three heroes right here in our classroom. Don't you think we should honor them?"

"Yeah," Billy couldn't resist adding. "Don't you?"

Alice Ann shrugged and opened her grammar book. "I suppose," she mumbled.

Billy, Finn, and Dannie looked at each other.

"Did you ever think we'd see the day when Miss Wrigley would hold us up as an example to Alice Ann?" Finn whispered.

Dannie grinned. "You know what? I may just end up liking it here in Scenic after all."

She hooked arms with Billy and Finn, and the three of them walked down the aisle to their desks.

Author's Note

I got the idea for the *Cascade Mountain Railroad Mysteries* from a surprising place—a calendar! A few years ago, my uncle, David Conroy, made the calendar as a present for our family. It was all about the building of the Cascade Tunnel in the 1920s. My grandfather was the general manager in charge of the project.

He took his family—my Grandma Conroy, Uncle Dave, and my mom—to live at the work-camp town in Scenic, Washington. Grandpa Conroy saved lots of photographs of the camp. My uncle used some of them in his calendar.

As soon as I saw the picture of the children standing outside Scenic's two-room schoolhouse (my uncle is the rascal in the white shirt in the second row, third from the right), I wanted to know more. More about the tunnel. More about the Scenic

camp. More about what it was
like to be a kid in Scenic back
then. I started asking a lot of
questions and doing research.
The result is *The Cascade Mountain
Railroad Mysteries.*

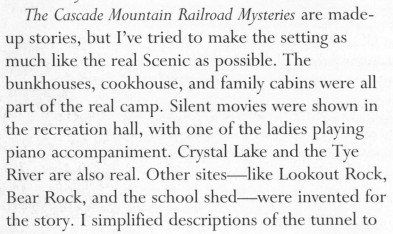

The Cascade Mountain Railroad Mysteries are made-
up stories, but I've tried to make the setting as
much like the real Scenic as possible. The
bunkhouses, cookhouse, and family cabins were all
part of the real camp. Silent movies were shown in
the recreation hall, with one of the ladies playing
piano accompaniment. Crystal Lake and the Tye
River are also real. Other sites—like Lookout Rock,
Bear Rock, and the school shed—were invented for
the story. I simplified descriptions of the tunnel to
keep the story from
getting too complicat-
ed. Also, I must admit
that the map of

the Scenic camp in this book is entirely made up! After three-quarters of a century, it is difficult to know exactly where everything was, but I have tried to capture the spirit of the place.

Why the Railroad Needed a Tunnel

Before the eight-mile Cascade Tunnel was built, crossing through the Cascade Mountains of Washington State was very dangerous, especially in the winter. Avalanches—giant snow slides—were a constant threat. To protect its passengers and trains, the Great Northern Railway built wooden shelters called snow sheds over the tracks. But the snow sheds weren't always enough. In 1910, an avalanche swept two trains off the tracks and 150 feet down into a canyon. 101 people were killed. Clearly, much better protection was needed.

Diagram of Cascade Tunnel route

Tunnels provided better shelter for the trains than snow sheds. A shorter tunnel, just 2.6 miles long, had already been built higher up the mountain. But the Great Northern Railway decided to build a new, longer tunnel lower down the mountainside, where snowslides were less of a danger. When the Cascade Tunnel was finished in 1929, it was the longest tunnel in the United States. It was called "a marvel of engineering skill" at the time it was built. At 8 miles, it is still one of the longest tunnels in the world today.

The Age of Radio

An early table model radio

In 1926, radio broadcasting was still in its early days. Television wouldn't become popular for more than twenty-five years! In the 1920s people all over the United States tuned in to local radio stations to hear music, sports events, presidential speeches, plays, lectures, and stories. One of the most popular radio shows was *Sam 'n' Henry*.

Sam 'n' Henry was a new kind of show—a radio comic strip that told a continuing story instead of entertaining listeners with music and jokes. The creators of the show, Charles Correll and Freeman

Gosden, acted out the lives of two Alabama men, Sam Smith and Henry Johnson. Listeners tuned in for ten minutes every night to follow Sam and Henry as they traveled to the big city of Chicago to find their fortunes. Everyone wanted to hear the daily adventures and troubles of their favorite characters. When Sam and Henry fell on hard times—losing their jobs and getting arrested for gambling—listeners wrote letters of sympathy to WGN, the Chicago radio station that broadcast the show.

Charles Correll and Freeman Gosden

Sam 'n' Henry was so popular that Charles Correll and Freeman Gosden used it as the model for a new show, *Amos 'n' Andy*. *Amos 'n' Andy* remained on the air for almost thirty years. The most popular radio show of all time, it later became a television series.

A Day in a Two-Room Schoolhouse

In 1926, most schools started at 9 A.M. and ended at 4 P.M. The day usually began with a prayer. Children in each grade worked on their lessons in

separate groups. The teacher moved from group to group, teaching lessons and then assigning work for the students to do while the teacher was busy working with the other groups.

Children studied reading, grammar, spelling, penmanship, math, history, and geography. Students also had to memorize and recite long speeches, poems, and literary passages. These recitations were done in the classroom and at community gatherings.

Kids playing marbles and hopscotch

The teachers often punished children who didn't obey the classroom rules. Students who misbehaved might have to skip recess or do extra chores, such as sweeping the floor or filling the coal bin. Sometimes the teachers slapped the hands of unruly students with a ruler.

During lunch and recess, kids played marbles, hop-scotch, leapfrog, and other games. Boys in Scenic played "chicken," balancing on logs in the Tye River and pushing each other until the loser fell in. They also played "war," using water-soaked pinecones as ammunition.

In 1926...

☛ The "flapper" style of bobbed haircuts and short skirts (just above the knee) was popular for girls.

☛ Knickers, boots, and flat caps were in style for boys.

☛ Sailor suits were worn by both girls and boys.

☛ Silent movies were all the rage. Charlie Chaplin, Buster Keaton, Rudolph Valentino, Lon Chaney, Harold Lloyd, and Clara Bow were some of the biggest box-office stars.

Kids in Scenic wore clothes like these.

☛ The *very* biggest movie star in 1926 was a dog! Rin Tin Tin was a German shepherd that was saved from a bombed-out kennel run by Germans in World War I. He was brought to the United States, where he starred in *The Courage of Rin Tin Tin* and other adventure movies.

Rin Tin Tin

☛ Gangster violence in Chicago was growing. It was illegal to buy or sell liquor during the Prohibition years. But alcoholic beverages were sold illegally on the black market. Al Capone's mob used threats and violence to take control of Chicago's bootleg liquor business. Gang violence was so bad that Chicago's business leaders begged the U.S. government to do something about it. Al Capone went to prison in 1932. He died in 1947.

Not everyone in Scenic owned an automobile.

About the Author

Anne Capeci has written many mysteries and other books for children, including titles in popular series such as *Wishbone Mysteries*, *Magic School Bus Science Chapter Books*, and *Mad Science*. Anne lives in Brooklyn, New York, with her husband and two children.